for Maddie, Piper and Riley – KC

To my mum, who is the best Grandma to my children.
Thank you for everything, Mum– LT

STRIPES PUBLISHING
An imprint of the Little Tiger Group
1 The Coda Centre, 189 Munster Road,
London SW6 6AW

A paperback original
First published in Great Britain in 2017

Text copyright © Katrina Charman, 2017
Illustrations copyright © Lucy Truman, 2017

ISBN: 978-1-84715-809-3

The right of Katrina Charman and Lucy Truman to be identified as
the author and illustrator of this work respectively has been asserted by
them in accordance with the Copyright, Designs and Patents Act, 1988.

Printed and bound in the UK.

10 9 8 7 6 5 4 3 2 1

# Poppy's Place

## THE GREAT CAT CAFÉ Rescue

ILLUSTRATED BY
LUCY TRUMAN

KATRINA CHARMAN

Stripes

Chapter
One

Abbey Park Vets was the busiest Isla had ever
seen it. She'd only popped in after school to
say a quick hello to her mum who worked
there as a veterinary nurse, but Mum had
looked so rushed off her feet that Isla offered
to stay and help.

"There's a bit of a wait, I'm afraid," Isla told
Mrs Jenkins, who had just arrived with her
labradoodle, Penny. "There was an emergency."

A little Yorkshire terrier had unexpectedly

run out into a road and been hit by a cyclist. Fortunately the cyclist was fine and the dog hadn't been too badly hurt but Lucy was running tests to make sure there were no broken bones or internal damage. *Unfortunately* the tests had taken quite a while and there was now a queue of pets waiting to be seen.

Mrs Jenkins stamped the snow from her boots then led Penny to an empty seat. Isla pressed the buzzer on the counter to let Mum know that another client had arrived, then pulled her notebook from her backpack.

Across the room Penny sniffed at a cardboard box on the floor containing Mr Kandu's tortoise, Shelby. Shelby wasn't fast on her feet at the best of times but today she had been brought in with a poorly front leg. She hobbled to the back of the box as quickly as she could to escape from Penny's slobber.

♡ 6 ♡

A door along the corridor opened and Mum appeared. As she hurried towards the waiting room, a pile of papers fluttered from her clipboard and scattered across the floor.

In the far corner, a lady Isla had never seen before desperately tried to keep hold of three bouncy border collie puppies, who clearly thought this was some kind of game. Isla rushed over to help Mum pick them up.

In front of the desk sat a boy called Jack who Isla recognized from school. He shifted awkwardly in his chair, repositioning the cage on his lap, which held a brightly coloured cockatiel. Isla held her hand up in a little wave but Jack looked down at the floor, his face flushing a bright shade of pink.

*That's strange*, Isla thought.

Mum followed Isla's gaze and gave her a little smile.

"Mrs Jenkins has just arrived for her four thirty appointment," Isla told Mum, handing her the last of the papers. "I told her you're running a bit behind."

"Thanks, Isla!" Mum said with a sigh, clipping the papers safely back into place. "Why do we always get emergencies on Fridays? Thank goodness you stopped by."

Isla smiled. "I'm happy to help."

Isla didn't tell Mum that the real reason she'd popped in was to avoid the huge maths project that she'd *still* not started. Isla thought it was really unfair to have been given homework to do over the holidays, so she'd decided to leave it until after Christmas. Then she'd waited until after New Year's Day … and now she'd already been back at school for a week and the project was due in next Friday! Luckily her friends Grace and Bonnie had the same project, so they'd made plans to finish it together at the weekend. Ayesha had offered to help, too, because she *loved* maths. Isla couldn't understand how anyone could love maths but she was grateful to her friend for helping them.

"Homework?" Mum asked, as though reading Isla's mind. She pointed to the open notebook in Isla's hand, which was covered in

Isla's cat doodles.

"Oh!" Isla shook her head. "No – I'm looking at my new year's resolutions."

The notebook was a Christmas present from Gran, and Isla's favourite notebook yet. It had a furry purple cover with a glittery black and white cat on the front. Isla thought the cat looked exactly like Poppy – their first forever cat.

"*Resolution number one,*" Isla read. "*Write more blog posts for our website.*"

Her older sister Tilda had created an amazing website for Poppy's Place, their cat café, and it was Isla's job to write profiles on the cats and keep the website up-to-date with news and events. But they'd been so busy over the Christmas holidays that Isla had barely even looked at it.

Mum glanced down at her watch. "As long

as none of your resolutions involves getting more cats!"

Isla paused. "Well, actually—"

The phone rang and Mum reached to answer it.

"Sorry, Isla," Mum interrupted, "I need to get this. We can chat later when it's a bit less hectic."

Isla sighed and closed her notebook. That's exactly what she'd wanted to talk to Mum about. But as they'd only just taken in Ash and Ace before Christmas, she knew it was unlikely that Mum would agree. Isla had hoped they would have rehomed more cats by now.

Mum held her hand over the receiver. "I almost forgot – could you take some cotton wool swabs to Lucy? She's in room two."

Isla went to the store cupboard, reaching up on tiptoes to pull a bag of extra-large cotton wool swabs off the top shelf. Then she hurried along to the examination room, wondering what kind of animal Lucy was treating. Isla hoped it was a cat, as long as it wasn't too badly injured or in pain.

"I've got these for you…" Isla trailed off as she saw the animal on the treatment table.

Isla had seen a lot of icky things during her time at Abbey Park – dogs with diarrhoea, infected wounds and broken legs. But she'd never seen anything quite as icky as the super-fluffy guinea pig Lucy was treating. Its face was covered with a half-sticky, half-crusty residue, and its nose gave a little whistle as it breathed in and out.

"Thank you, Isla," Lucy said, taking the bag of swabs. "Could you fill a bowl with warm water for me, please?"

Isla filled a metal bowl, making sure that the

water wasn't too hot, and passed it to Lucy.

"Jasper's nose won't stop running," the guinea pig's owner, a boy of about Isla's age, told her. "It's getting *everywhere.*"

"Don't worry," Lucy said. "We'll have him cleaned up in no time. And I'll give you some medicine to dry up his nose."

Isla laughed as Jasper let out a little sneeze.

"It wouldn't be so bad if it wasn't for all this hair!" Lucy said as she used the cotton wool swabs to clean
the guinea pig's
fur. It stuck up
at all angles,
making him
look like a huge
furry football
rather than a
small rodent.

A few minutes later, Jasper and his owner were on their way home.

"How's the waiting room?" Lucy asked.

"Still packed," Isla replied.

"Animals are a bit like humans," Lucy said, washing her hands. "They often get more illnesses in the winter. And how's everything going at Poppy's Place?"

"We've been fully booked every weekend since we opened," Isla said proudly. "Even on Christmas Eve. But Mum insisted that we closed over New Year – just to give everyone a break."

"I think you're doing a fabulous job," Lucy told Isla. "And the cats all seem very happy and healthy."

Isla beamed. It felt amazing to have Lucy – who was an animal expert – say that they were doing a great job.

"The cats love all the attention," Isla replied. "Especially Poppy – she's always showing off her tricks. Even Oliver wakes up for a cuddle every now and then!" Isla frowned for a moment. "It's just … I thought we'd have helped more cats find new homes by now," she admitted.

Isla loved having a house full of cats but part of the reason they'd opened a cat café was to help homeless cats find their forever homes. So far, they'd rehomed Victoria and Albert, who had been adopted at Christmas, and three of Benny's kittens. Isla knew there were lots more cats in need of their help.

Mum appeared in the doorway with Jack's cockatiel. "Jack said he'd wait outside," she told Lucy, glancing sideways at Isla.

"What's that look for?" Isla asked.

Mum shook her head quickly. "Nothing…

I just think Jack might have a little crush on you."

Isla felt her face go hot. "On *me*?"

"Anyway," Mum said with a grin, "Dolly's here with one of the cats from the sanctuary, if you want to say hello."

Isla hurried back to the waiting room, avoiding making eye contact with Jack as she passed the desk. Isla didn't know what her mum was talking about – of *course* Jack didn't have a crush on her! He was probably just embarrassed about being seen with a cockatiel – they weren't the coolest of pets.

"Hi, Isla!" Dolly smiled. "It's been a while since I've seen you. How are Poppy's Place's newest arrivals getting on?"

Ash and Ace had come from Dolly's Farm, where she ran a sanctuary for homeless and unwanted cats.

"They've settled in really well," Isla said. "They especially love the cat playground in the garden – even in this weather!"

Isla nodded to the cat carrier Dolly was holding. "Who do you have in there? Is it a new cat?"

Dolly held up the carrier so that Isla could see inside. A small tortoiseshell cat was curled into a ball, shivering. "He came in on Boxing Day, would you believe! An unwanted Christmas present."

"That's awful!" Isla cried.

Having a pet was a big responsibility. Isla couldn't understand why people thought animals were just things to be bought and given away.

"Ah! He's gorgeous, poor thing. What's wrong with him?" Isla asked.

"I'm not sure," said Dolly. "He's not eating his food and he's already underweight. I was hoping Lucy could take a quick look." She glanced around the waiting room. "I wasn't expecting it to be this busy, though."

"We had an emergency earlier, so we're running a bit behind," Isla explained.

Mum reappeared from the treatment room. "Lucy said she can fit you in, if you don't mind a bit of a wait," she said. "Will you be taking him back to the sanctuary?"

Dolly nodded. "For now, although I haven't

really got room for him," she admitted.

Isla's heart sank. "But where will he go if he can't stay at yours?"

Dolly glanced at Mum before answering. "I'm not sure, Isla. I've taken on a few more cats than I can really cope with lately because I just can't bear to turn them away, but there comes a point when even I have to say no."

"We could have more at Poppy's Place, couldn't we, Mum?" Isla suggested.

"We have to find Ash and Ace their forever homes first," Mum replied gently. "And that could take a while. I'm sorry, Isla – we can't take any more cats for the moment."

Dolly gave Isla a small smile. "Your mum's right. We just have to face facts, I'm afraid – until I rehome some of the existing cats, I won't be able to take in any more."

Isla gasped. "But what will happen to all the

other unwanted cats?" she asked in a shaky voice.

Dolly shook her head. "I don't know, Isla. I'm going to try to make contact with another sanctuary to see if they have space. That's the best I can do for now."

Isla looked at the little cat inside the carrier. There had to be a way to rehome more of the cats, Isla thought. She just needed to find it.

## Chapter Two

Isla woke early on Saturday morning to a loud thumping noise outside her bedroom door. She felt like she'd hardly slept. She'd lain awake for ages, trying to come up with a way to help Dolly. When she'd finally fallen asleep, she'd had nightmares about hundreds of homeless kittens wandering the streets. Dolly had told her not to worry but Isla still wished there was something she could do to help.

The thumping noise started again. Isla put

on her glasses and stumbled out on to the landing.

"What's going on?" she asked her sister.

Tilda was coming down the attic stairs from her room, hauling the biggest backpack Isla had ever seen.

"I'm going hiking, remember? For my Duke of Edinburgh Award."

Isla glanced out of the window at the slush-covered ground and shivered. "You're not camping, are you? Mum said there might be more snow this weekend."

"If the weather gets too bad, we're going to stay in a youth hostel," Tilda explained. "Anyway, it might be fun if it snows."

Isla wasn't convinced. She didn't think Tilda looked entirely happy about it either.

"Are you sure you need to take that much with you?" Gran asked, coming to join them.

"You're only going for one night," Isla said, rolling her eyes behind Tilda's back.

Gran tried to hide her smile but not before Tilda had seen it. She spun round to glare at Isla.

"I *do*, actually," Tilda said. She waved a piece of paper in the air. "You're not the only one who can make a list, Isla."

A car horn beeped outside. "That's my lift!" said Tilda. She dragged her bag along the floor, heading for the stairs. "I'll see you tomorrow night!"

"Have fun!" Gran called after her.

"I'm not sure I'd want to be camping in this weather," Isla said. "And how is Tilda going to hike with that backpack if she can't even lift it off the ground?"

Gran sighed. "She'll probably convince some poor boy to carry it, knowing Tilda. Anyway we haven't got time to worry about that now. Your mum's taken Milo to his friend Joe's house for the morning. So could you make a start on setting up the café? We're fully booked this morning."

Isla's little brother Milo loved cats almost as much as she did, but his hearing aid meant that he sometimes found the constant noise of the café a bit difficult and it made him grumpy about having to share the cats (and his home) with all the café's customers. Isla knew how he felt. Sometimes she wished it was just her and all the cats.

Isla nodded and let out another big yawn. "My friends are coming over later to work on our maths project, but if you need us to do anything, let me know."

"I might take you up on that. Especially if your mum gets called into the vets," Gran said. She gave a small sigh. "I'd better start baking."

Isla frowned. Gran was usually never happier than when she was baking but lately she didn't seem to be enjoying it as much. She watched Gran disappear into the kitchen with Poppy following behind. Gran's baking was part of what made their cat café so popular.

Isla hated to see her looking so fed up. *I'll chat to Mum about Gran later*, Isla thought.

After a quick breakfast, Isla changed into her Poppy's Place T-shirt and jeans, and got to work. She grabbed a handful of cutlery and a pile of napkins from the kitchen and headed into the conservatory, being careful not to step on any cat tails.

The conservatory was set up with tables and chairs and a couple of comfy sofas. The large windows that looked out on to the garden were white with frost and the sky outside was dark grey. Isla turned up the radiators so that the cats (and the café) would be warm and cosy.

As Isla set to work, she heard a little meow

and a moment
later Roo
wriggled through
the cat flap. Isla
kneeled down to
tickle his tummy.

"Sorry, Roo,"
Isla said. "I don't
have time to play this morning."

She glanced over at the fence to see if there
was any sign of her neighbour, Sam, who was
usually outside kicking his football around.
"Probably too cold, even for him," Isla told Roo.

When they'd gone to school together, Isla
had thought that Sam was a bit of a pain. But
now they were at different secondary schools,
she missed talking to him.

Isla settled Roo on one of the sofas and
finished setting the tables. As she headed back

to the kitchen, Isla breathed in deeply, giving Gran two thumbs up. "Smells delicious," she said, as Gran spread thick vanilla icing over a coffee and walnut cake.

Gran waved Isla away. "That's not for you! If you've finished laying the tables, how about helping me with the washing up? I'm already behind with my cupcakes."

Isla looked over at the stack of mixing bowls and baking tins in the sink and groaned.

"You could do with an assistant," Isla said, plunging her hands into the soapy water. "Bonnie loves to bake."

"Does she know how to work the coffee machine?" Gran asked hopefully.

Isla laughed. The coffee machine had become Gran's arch-enemy ever since the milk frother had exploded all over her. Isla had even overheard Gran trying to convince customers to order a pot of tea rather than a latte so she wouldn't have to use it.

"How do you think Tilda will get on with the hiking?" Isla said.

Gran pulled a tray of freshly baked rolls out of the oven. "She'll probably be too busy on her phone to notice anything around her. I just hope she doesn't get lost because she's not paying attention to where she's going."

Isla snorted. "At least she can use the GPS on her phone to find her way home – if there's any signal."

Isla had been quite surprised when Tilda had announced the camping trip last week. Her sister usually hated doing outdoorsy stuff, *especially* in the middle of winter. Unless it involved camping outside her favourite clothes shop when they had a sale on.

Gran checked her watch. "I'll finish that,

Isla. Can you spoon the cupcake mixture into these cases for me?" Gran asked, brushing flour from the front of her apron.

Isla gratefully dried her hands and took over from Gran, making sure that she didn't drip any of the mixture over the sides.

The front door opened and Mum hurried inside, stamping her feet. "My toes are numb!" she cried. "How's everything going here?"

"We're nearly there," Gran said. "Isla's set the tables, and the cupcakes are just about to go into the oven."

Isla spooned the last of the mixture into a paper case, then licked the spoon clean. She reached for her notebook, which was sitting on the kitchen table. "If you don't need me, I'm going to write profiles for Ash and Ace before Bonnie, Grace and Ayesha arrive. We need to find them their forever home so we can take more of Dolly's cats."

Gran smiled. "I think we're all set, thanks."

Isla headed into the conservatory and settled down on a beanbag beside the new cats. They were curled up together on a fluffy cat bed that hung over the top of the radiator.

"I'm not sure that's meant for more than one cat!" Isla giggled.

Roo popped out from beneath a sofa cushion and jumped on to Isla's lap, batting a paw at her pen.

"Do you want to help?" Isla asked, pulling the pen away from Roo's tiny teeth.

*Ash and Ace are brothers,* Isla wrote. *They are about two years old and have never had a real home of their own. They were found abandoned behind a Chinese takeaway in the city. They have beautiful black fur and piercing green eyes. When they are not sleeping,* (which is often, Isla thought) *they love playing together and need lots of cuddles and attention. Ace especially loves tummy rubs.*

There was a knock at the front door and Gran called Isla from the kitchen. Isla quickly scribbled a final note. *Ash and Ace should go to a home where they can stay together.*

Isla shut her notebook and ran to greet her friends.

"It's freezing out there!" Grace shrieked, placing her icy hands on Isla's face.

"Argh!" Isla squealed, leaping away. "Get your hands off me!"

Grace, Bonnie and Ayesha followed Isla into the kitchen. "Hot chocolate?" Isla suggested.

Ayesha nodded eagerly. "Yes, please!"

While the girls sipped their hot chocolate, Isla told her friends about the problems at Dolly's sanctuary. "I wish I could find a way to

help Dolly rehome the cats faster," she said.
"Otherwise she won't be able to take in any
more."

"That's so sad," Bonnie said. "Couldn't you
have some more here?"

"That's what I suggested," Isla said loudly
as Mum walked by with an armful of table
decorations.

Mum shook her head. "And I said no! We
haven't got room for any more cats."

Isla sighed. Mum was right – they had
Poppy, Benny and Roo, who were the Palmers'
forever cats, along with Dynamo – one of
Benny's kittens and Milo's favourite. They had
also taken on an old ginger cat called Oliver
from Dolly's sanctuary, and now they had Ash
and Ace as well.

Isla glanced over at Grace and Bonnie as
they whispered something to each other.

Suddenly, they burst out laughing.

"What's so funny?" Isla asked.

"Nothing!" Bonnie cried, putting her hand over Grace's mouth.

Grace wriggled free. "Bonnie wants to ask someone at school to go with her to the Valentine's disco," Grace said, with a sly grin.

"Grace! That was a secret," Bonnie squealed. "I said *maybe* it would be nice if someone asked me to go with them."

"Who?" Isla asked.

Bonnie suddenly became engrossed in her hot chocolate while Grace nudged her shoulder.

"I wish we had a Valentine's disco at my school," Ayesha said.

Isla, Bonnie and Grace went to Langford High, but Ayesha went to a private school on the other side of the city.

"It's going to be amazing!" Grace gushed. "I've already decided what I'm going to wear – well, almost. I'm thinking either my purple dress with the long flowy skirt, or the strapless pink one with sequins. What are you going to wear, Isla?"

Isla shrugged. "I hadn't really thought about it." It wasn't that Isla didn't like discos, she just didn't really enjoy the drama that went with them – deciding on what to wear, worrying about dancing in front of people…

Bonnie gasped. "We'll help you. *Everyone's* going to be there."

*But not Ayesha*, Isla thought. She wondered if they were allowed to bring friends to the disco.

"Customers!" Gran called. "Time to make yourselves scarce, girls!"

"Head up to my room," Isla told her friends. "I'm going to help welcome the customers then I'll be right up. You can make a start on the maths project."

Grace and Bonnie let out loud groans as they hurried upstairs with Ayesha. Isla went to the front door to help Mum greet the guests. They only allowed up to twelve people at a time in the café so the cats wouldn't be too overwhelmed.

"I'll show them to their tables, if you like?" Isla offered.

"Thanks," Mum said. "I'll go and make sure Gran is OK – she looks a bit frazzled."

After greeting the customers, Isla led them to the downstairs bathroom so that they could wash their hands. Lucy said this was important to prevent any infections being spread – to humans or cats.

The customers chatted excitedly while they waited, asking Isla questions about the café and all the cats.

When they were finished, Isla showed them to their tables. The last people to be seated were a lady and her young daughter who looked about seven or eight.

"Someone will be through soon to take your order," Isla told them. "We do have a few rules." She pointed to a sign hanging on the wall. "Let the cats come to you. You can use anything in there to see if they want to play."

Isla gestured to a basket of cat toys nearby.

The little girl hurried over to the basket. Inside were small fishing rods with feathers, balls of wool and Dynamo's favourite – a torch. Dynamo loved chasing the beam of light across the floor.

Poppy padded over to the little girl and rubbed her nose against the girl's hand.

"I think Poppy wants to play!" Isla smiled.

"Ava has read all about Poppy on your website," the girl's mum told Isla. "And watched the videos. She's a huge fan."

"If you hold your hand up, Poppy might give you a high five," Isla told Ava.

Ava held out her hand and Poppy batted at it with her paw. "This is the best place ever!" she squealed excitedly.

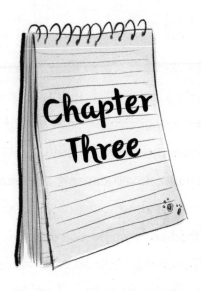

## Chapter Three

It was Sunday afternoon. Isla stared at her maths project and sighed. Even with Ayesha's help, they hadn't managed to get it all done yesterday because Bonnie and Grace had talked non-stop about the Valentine's disco. Isla groaned and made a mental note to never leave homework until Sunday ever again. She had planned to finish it earlier in the day, but Poppy's Place had been fully booked in the morning, so she and Milo had helped out as much as they could. Then she'd started trying to work on a plan to solve Dolly's cat problem. Except she couldn't think of anything and after an hour the page was still blank, so she'd given up and reluctantly opened her maths book.

She stared at the final question, which was all about probability, and was just wondering what the probability would be that she'd get the project finished on time, when an ear-splitting shriek rang through the air.

"ARGHHHHHH!"

Isla ran downstairs to find Milo rolling around on the hall carpet, clutching at his stomach.

"What's wrong?" Isla cried. "Are you hurt?" She kneeled down beside him, looking for any injuries. She couldn't see any blood, but Milo was making a weird huffing noise.

Isla paused for a moment, then leaned in

closer. "Are you … laughing?"

Milo sat up, still clutching his stomach as he let out a great big whoop of laughter. He pointed in the direction of the lounge.

"It's. Not. Funny. Milo!" Tilda growled, emerging from the lounge. She was covered from head to toe in thick, congealed mud.

"It's the swamp monster!" Milo howled.

"Um … what…" Isla spluttered, trying her best not to laugh. "What happened to you?"

"There was a bog," Tilda said, through gritted teeth.

"And you decided to swim in it?" Isla asked.

"Is everything all right?" Gran called, hurrying into the hallway from the kitchen with Mum hot on her heels. She spotted Tilda and stopped so suddenly that Mum crashed into her.

"Oh dear!" said Gran, holding a hand up to her mouth.

Mum peered round Gran and took in the scene. "Just look at the carpet!" she cried, shaking her head at the muddy trail of footprints that led into the lounge from the front door. "It's covered in mud!"

"Never mind that!" Tilda shrieked. "Look at my hair! It's going to take me forever to wash all the mud out."

"You'd better make a start then," Mum replied. "And as soon as you're done, you can come and clean up this mess."

"I'm going to get my camera!" Milo teased.

"Don't you dare!" Tilda hissed.

"I'll make a path for you," Gran said. "We don't want you trailing mud upstairs." She laid out plastic bags on the floor, leading all the way up to the bathroom.

Isla tried to look as sympathetic as she could as Tilda stomped past, only to burst into laughter at the last second when she was unable to hold it in any longer. Tilda gave Isla the sort of glare that meant Isla would regret laughing later, but she decided that the vision of a less-than-perfect Tilda made it worth it.

"Can I come in?" Tilda asked, knocking at Isla's bedroom door. She peered into the room.

Isla jolted awake and sat up with a start. One of the pages of her maths project was stuck to the side of her face. "I must have fallen asleep," she groaned, peeling the paper carefully away from her cheek. She looked at Tilda. "You look much better."

Her hair was wrapped in a towel and she was wearing a pair of cosy-looking pyjamas.

Tilda grinned. "You should see the state of the bath."

"So, you didn't have a very good weekend?" Isla asked.

"It was actually quite fun," Tilda admitted. "Until the bog incident. I didn't see the mud until I'd stepped right in it. It took three people to pull me out!" She gave Isla a little smile. "How was your weekend?"

"Busy," Isla said, holding up her notebook. "I'm working on a plan to help Dolly but I'm not getting very far." She sighed. "And I've still not finished my maths project, and the café was fully booked. Everyone's been working flat out – I'm almost jealous of you going on a hike, even in this weather!"

Tilda gave Isla a sympathetic nod. "Can I tell you a secret?" she whispered. "One of the reasons I signed up to do the Duke of Edinburgh Award was to give myself a bit of a break from Poppy's Place."

Isla opened her mouth to reply but Tilda interrupted before she could speak.

"Don't get me wrong," Tilda said. "I love Poppy's Place and everything we're doing here, but I just –" she sighed – "I don't have as much time to see my friends any more, and I've got exams coming up, and…" She broke off, looking down at the floor. "Running a cat café is a lot harder than I'd thought it would be."

Isla nodded. "I know what you mean. Gran's baking *all* the time and she seemed really fed up yesterday. And if Mum's not working at the vets, she's working here. She never has a day off. But what can we do? If we tell Mum, she might close Poppy's Place. What will happen to the cats who still need homes?"

"Maybe if we talk to her together, we can come up with some ideas. Family meeting?" Tilda suggested.

Isla felt terrible. It had been her idea to open the cat café in the first place. She hated the thought that it was taking over their lives, but she didn't want Mum to give up on

Poppy's Place either – especially not now Dolly was having to turn cats away at the sanctuary. There had to be another solution.

Isla nodded. "Let's get everyone together in the conservatory," she said.

Five minutes later, the whole family was assembled. Milo wandered in, wearing his favourite superhero outfit and carrying Dynamo around in his arms like a baby, followed by Mum and Gran. They were joined by most of the cats as well.

"What's this about, Isla?" Gran asked. "I've got to get the chicken out of the oven in a minute."

"It won't take long," Isla promised. She took a shaky breath. "Since we opened Poppy's Place, everyone's been so busy and it seems like some of the fun has gone out of it."

Isla glanced at Gran. "Gran, you don't seem

to enjoy baking as much as you used to."

Gran nodded thoughtfully. "It does seem more like hard work than fun these days," she admitted. "It's not that I don't enjoy baking – just maybe not baking every day!"

"We knew it would be hard, Isla," Mum said.

"I know," Isla replied. "But when you're not working at the vets, you're working here."

Milo nodded. "We don't go anywhere any more."

"Our friends have been helping out now and then, but maybe we need something a bit more permanent?" Isla said.

"Perhaps we could hire someone?" Tilda suggested. "We're making a bit of a profit now." She paused as she looked at Mum. "I'm not going to be able to help as much with my exams coming up, and it might give you and Gran a little break?"

Mum was quiet for a while, then she turned to Gran. "What do you think?"

"I think it's a great idea," said Gran. "We'd only need someone part time."

"And maybe we could have one day each month when we're closed at the weekend so we can have some family time," Isla said, looking at Milo.

"I was just about to suggest that!" said Mum.

"Can we go to the zoo?" Milo asked. "I keep asking but you're always too busy."

Mum gave Milo a hug. "Of course we can!"

Tilda stood up. "I can design an advert for the website now, if you like? Oh, or a video – Poppy can be the star!"

"Hold on!" Mum said, waving a hand at Tilda. "It's not that simple. I'm sure there are forms to fill in if we want to employ someone, and other things to think about…"

"But surely we can at least advertise for someone in the meantime?" said Tilda. "It will probably take forever for people to apply anyway."

Isla wasn't so sure. She would jump at the chance to work in a cat café – if she didn't already *live* in one.

"OK, you can make a start," Mum agreed. "But don't post it on the website until I say so."

"There's something else I wanted to discuss," Isla said.

Tilda rolled her eyes and flopped back down on to her beanbag. Her phone beeped with a text. She pulled it out of her pyjama pocket, blushing as she read the message on the screen.

Isla narrowed her eyes suspiciously at Tilda, then continued.

"It's important!" she said, opening her notebook. She found the plan she'd been working on before she'd fallen asleep: *Save the cats!* Then she remembered that it was still blank. She sighed. She'd just have to speak from the heart.

"We opened Poppy's Place to find homes

for all the cats out there like Poppy. She didn't have a home until we took her in," Isla started. Poppy meowed as though in agreement. "But…"

Tilda's phone beeped again. "Sorry!" she said, giggling as she read another text.

Isla glanced over at Mum, who rolled her eyes.

"As I was saying," Isla continued. "There are still so many cats at Dolly's Farm who deserve a forever home just like Poppy. But Dolly needs help – the farm is full to bursting and she can't take in any more." She gave her mum a pleading look.

Mum shook her head. "Oh, no. I've already told you we can't take in any more cats, Isla."

"I know," Isla said quickly, "but there must be something we can do." She tapped her pen on her notebook, trying to think of a solution.

Suddenly she remembered Grace and Bonnie and their hopes for the Valentine's disco and gasped. "We could do something for Valentine's Day! A love match between the cats at the sanctuary and potential owners. I'm sure that would help find homes for some of the cats and then Dolly would have space to take in more!"

"We could have it here at Poppy's Place," Tilda added. "It would be great publicity."

"I don't know, Isla," said Gran. "It sounds like an awful lot of work."

"Since when has hard work stopped us?" Isla said. "We can do it. I know we can! I'm sure our friends will help out…" Isla looked at Mum. "Think of all the cats at the sanctuary and out on the streets – don't they deserve a home?"

Mum sighed. "I'll have to talk to Dolly first,

to see if she thinks it's a good idea."

Isla grinned and clapped her hands. "She will! I know she will." She started frantically making notes in her notebook. "This is going to be perfect! We can call it The Great Cat-tacular!"

She jumped up to give Mum a hug, startling Ash and Ace who were curled up on the radiator hammock beside her. "What could possibly go wrong?"

## Chapter Four

Nothing could spoil Isla's good mood as she trudged home from school on Monday afternoon. Not the freezing sleet that had soaked through her shoes and turned her toes to ice. Not the fact that *all* Grace and Bonnie had talked about for the entire day was the Valentine's disco. Not even the huge ladder she had running down her tights from Roo attaching himself to her leg that morning.

The more she thought about her idea to

help Dolly find some of the cats new homes, the more certain she was that it would work. She had made so many plans and notes throughout the day that her new notebook was almost full. As she passed the parade of shops at the bottom of her road, she read through everything she'd written so far.

# The Great Cat-tacular!

## What?

An all-day event where potential cat owners can find out all about the cats available for adoption at Poppy's Place and Dolly's Farm.

## Where?

Poppy's Place Cat Café, Abbey Park.

## When?

Saturday, 14th February.
Valentine's Day! 11 – 3 p.m.

Isla squealed in excitement. It was absolutely perfect. If they could get anywhere near the same amount of people attending the Cat-tacular as they'd had come to the Poppy's Place launch party, she was sure they would find loads of cats their forever homes.

"Have you spoken to Dolly yet?" Isla called out as soon as she arrived home.

She found Mum and Gran in the kitchen, enjoying a cup of tea and a slice of Victoria sponge.

"Hi, Mum, hi, Gran," Mum said in a weird high-pitched voice that did not sound at *all* like Isla. "Have you had a good day?"

Isla rolled her eyes. "Hi, Mum, hi, Gran," she said, giving them both a quick hug. "Have you had a good day?"

Milo zoomed into the kitchen from out of

nowhere and shouted "Hi, Isla!" before grabbing the biggest slice of cake and zooming back out.

"Milo!" Gran tutted. "At least take a napkin with you."

Isla helped herself to a slice of cake and put it on a plate so that she wouldn't get a telling-off from Gran, then she sat down next to Mum. Aside from the cats, Isla's favourite thing about running a cat café was Gran's baking. The house had a permanent scent of cinnamon and icing and chocolate.

"So…" Isla mumbled with her mouth full of cake. "Have you spoken to Dolly about The Great Cat-tacular?"

Mum looked at Isla and took a long sip of tea. Then she slowly put the teacup down and paused before lifting it to her lips again.

"Mum!" Isla cried.

Mum grinned. "Yes, Isla. I've spoken to Dolly."

"And…" Isla said, barely able to sit still.

"And she thinks it's a great idea," Mum said. "Lucy does, too. She's offered to come to the event to give advice to potential cat owners – about immunizations, insurance, neutering. And the cost."

"That's perfect!" Isla said, adding Lucy's name to her list of helpers. "That way we can be sure that the cats find the best homes."

Isla heard a shuffle and a small giggle out in the corridor. Milo poked his head into the kitchen.

"Where are we going to put all the cats?" he asked.

"What do you mean?" Isla said.

"For the great spec … cat … ular," he said.

"*Cat*-tacular!" Isla huffed. "Honestly it's not

that difficult to remember."

"They won't actually come here," Mum told Milo. "There are far too many cats at the sanctuary to bring them all to Poppy's Place."

"But … then how will people be able to choose which cat they want to adopt?" Milo asked.

"Good point," said Gran.

Isla frowned. It hadn't occurred to her that they wouldn't be able to bring Dolly's cats to Poppy's Place.

"Maybe Dolly could bring a few of the cats who could cope with being around lots of people, and we could take photos of the other cats available for adoption. I can write their profiles and upload them to the website. Then we can hand out profile sheets on the day while people meet the cats here at Poppy's Place, and chat with Lucy and Dolly."

Gran laughed. "It sounds like Isla's got it all figured out!"

Isla tapped her notebook with her pen. "There's still a lot to organize, though," she said. She flipped through her notebook – *refreshments, helpers, decorations, promotion, posters* – the list went on and on.

Isla looked at the cat calendar stuck to the front of the fridge. There were three full weeks until Valentine's Day. She hoped they would be able to get everything ready in time – there were cats counting on her.

The week flew by with school, homework and making plans for The Great Cat-tacular. Mum had filled in Dolly on their idea and had arranged for Isla to go to the sanctuary to

write cat profiles and take photos on Saturday
morning. As soon as Mum got home from
work on Friday, Isla showed her the advert
she and Tilda had been working on for a
part-time helper at Poppy's Place. Tilda had
taken a really cute photograph of Poppy
performing one of her newest tricks –
standing up on her hind legs.

# Help Wanted!
## at Poppy's Place

We're looking for some part-time help in our
cat café. Experience helpful and must love cats!
Click here for further details.

"What do you think?" Isla asked. "I'm sure we'll get loads of people applying. Who wouldn't want to work at a cat café? Shall we fix a date for the interviews? And maybe we should get some more Poppy's Place T-shirts made so all the staff wear the same thing, and—"

"Hang on, Isla!" Mum said. "I'm not sure I have time to interview staff at the moment, what with work and Poppy's Place and The Great Cat-palooza!"

"Cat-*tacular*," Isla corrected. "And I've already told you that you don't have to worry about that." She held up her notebook. "I've got everything under control."

Mum glanced at Isla's notebook and frowned.

"So … can we post the advert on the website?" Isla asked. "Tilda thought we could print some copies to put up in the conservatory and at Abbey Park Vets."

Mum nodded. "All right, I suppose so," she said. "We do need help."

"We might even have some applicants this weekend," Isla said.

"Don't get your hopes up, Isla," Mum warned. "It could take a while."

Isla ran up to Tilda's attic room where she found her sister engrossed in her laptop.

"Mum said yes!" Isla told Tilda. "You can upload the advert to the website."

"Already done," Tilda said with a grin.

Isla stared. "Tilda!"

"Don't give me that look," said Tilda. "I knew Mum would say yes – she always does. I've uploaded a new video of Poppy performing her latest trick, too."

"We should start on the advert for the

Cat-tacular," Isla said.

"I've already done that as well," Tilda said, spinning her laptop round so that Isla could see the screen. "Well, I've written a blog post about it."

"That was my job!" Isla huffed.

"You can still design the poster," said Tilda. She grabbed her phone as it vibrated on her bedside table. She swiped her thumb across the screen and smiled.

"Who keeps texting you?" Isla asked, leaning over Tilda's shoulder for a peek. It wasn't unusual for Tilda to be glued to her phone but lately she seemed to be even more obsessed with it.

Tilda blushed and shoved her phone in her jeans pocket. "None of your business!" she snapped. "It was just Gabriella asking me about … a thing."

Isla waited for Tilda to say more about the *thing* but she ignored Isla and went back to her laptop.

"Maybe if you helped Mum and Gran a bit more instead of staring at your phone, they wouldn't be run off their feet!" Isla grumbled.

"Well, maybe if you weren't always writing lists, you could help more, too!" Tilda shot back.

Isla folded her arms across her chest and glared at Tilda while she glared back in silence. After a bit Tilda sighed. "Let's not fall out. I'm sure we can both do a little more to help out."

Isla nodded. Tilda was right – there was so much to do with Poppy's Place and the Cat-tacular that they didn't have time to argue. From now until Valentine's Day, the Cat-tacular and the cats were all that mattered.

## Chapter Five

On Saturday morning, Isla and Mum caught
the first bus to Dolly's Farm. Isla felt a bit
guilty about leaving Gran and Tilda behind to
deal with the customers at Poppy's Place, but
she needed to write profiles for every cat at
the sanctuary and the only way she could do
that was by actually visiting them and talking
to Dolly.

"I hope Milo won't be too upset when he
finds out where we've gone," Isla said.

Mum sighed. "He'll be OK. I'm sure he'll have more fun bowling with his friends than he will at the cat sanctuary."

"I'm not so sure," Isla replied. "He loves Dolly's alpacas."

The cat sanctuary was part of Dolly's Farm, which meant that the cats had loads of space to roam rather than being stuck in cages. Dolly did an amazing job caring for the cats and all the other animals, but it wasn't the same as having a real owner, Isla thought. Or a real home.

As they got off the bus and walked to the farm, Mum's phone beeped.

"Bad timing," Mum told Isla. "It's Lucy. She needs me to come into work for a bit."

"Oh," Isla said. "Does that mean I won't be able to write the cat profiles?"

Mum gave Isla an apologetic smile. "I'm afraid not."

"Hi, you two," Dolly called, as Isla and Mum walked up the gravel path towards the farm. "Why so glum?"

"We can't stay," Isla said. "Mum's been called into work."

"I'm sorry, Isla," Mum said. "I can't leave you here – I wouldn't want you making the journey home all by yourself."

"I could bring her home," Dolly suggested. "I was going to pop by the vets today to see Lucy anyway – she wanted to do a follow-up with the cat I brought in last week."

"Oh, can she?" Isla asked Mum, hopefully.

Mum looked at Dolly. "Well, if you're sure?"

Dolly nodded. "No problem! We've got a lot of work to do for The Great Cat-tacular, haven't we, Isla?"

Isla pulled her notebook and pen out of her backpack. "Ready when you are!"

Mum said a quick goodbye, then Dolly and Isla set off around the farm with Dolly pointing out the cats, and telling Isla their names and background story if she knew it.

"Some of these cats were just dumped at the gate," Dolly said.

Dolly pointed at a dark grey cat sitting on top of the chicken coop. "That's Sylvie," Dolly told Isla. "She's a very special cat."

"Why?" Isla asked.

Dolly called out Sylvie's name. Sylvie stood up, arching her back with a big yawn before jumping down to wander over to Isla and Dolly.

Isla gasped. "She's only got three legs!"

"It doesn't seem to bother her at all, though," Dolly said, kneeling down to tickle Sylvie behind the ear.

Isla kneeled down, too, and Sylvie rubbed against her leg, purring loudly.

"You should see her tease those chickens," Dolly chuckled. "She's just as fast as some of the other cats."

"What happened to her?" Isla asked.

"I'm not sure," Dolly said. "She came from another cat sanctuary. I think she was probably born with three legs."

"She's amazing," Isla breathed, scratching Sylvie's head.

"Don't forget to make notes," Dolly reminded Isla with a smile.

"I could sit here with Sylvie all day," Isla said. "I really hope we can find homes for some of these cats."

"Me too, Isla," Dolly said. "But whatever happens, you're doing a wonderful thing. Thank you."

Isla spent the rest of the morning with Dolly and the cats, until it was time to head back to Abbey Park. Dolly had nineteen cats altogether and Isla made as many notes as she could about each one. Tilda had let Isla borrow her camera to take photos of them all and, as she made her way around the farm, snapping away at the cats, she couldn't help but feel a bubble of worry in her stomach – what if nobody came to the Cat-tacular? What would happen to the cats then?

By the time Isla got home, the morning guests had already left and Poppy's Place was empty.

"How did it go?" Tilda asked, as Isla poked her head into the conservatory.

"Good," Isla said. "I think I got pictures of all of the cats – although some of them wouldn't stay still for a close-up!"

Tilda laughed as she wiped down the last of the tables. "I think Milo's sulking about missing out on the farm," she said. "He hasn't left his room since he got home."

Isla frowned. "I'll tell him he can come with me next time."

"Right," said Tilda. "I'm just about done here. Shall we have a look at the photos? I can start uploading them to the website before the afternoon customers arrive."

"Great," Isla said. "I want to check our emails as well, in case anyone has applied for the job."

Tilda fetched her laptop and downloaded

the pictures of Dolly's cats as Isla told her about Sylvie. Then she passed Isla the laptop to read the emails and reached for her phone.

Isla was just scrolling through the messages when her phone beeped. She reached into her pocket and pulled it out. There was a text from Grace asking what she was thinking about doing with her hair for the disco. Isla sighed and switched her phone to silent. She loved Grace but at the moment all she could think about was the disco.

"We've had three applications already!" Isla said, returning to the emails. "Listen to this one – she used to work at an animal shelter, loves cats, has waitressing experience."

"Sounds good." Tilda nodded.

"Oh, but wait!" Isla said as she read through the next application. "This one actually worked at a cat café when she lived in Japan!"

"Impressive," Tilda mumbled, as she tapped out a text on her phone.

Isla glanced over at Tilda and frowned. "This one says she worked on the cat space station and has a degree in cat-ology. Her name is *Cat*erina Catterson."

"That's perfect," Tilda said, as her phone beeped. "Wait… What was that last one?"

Isla shook her head. This was exactly what she'd been talking about last night – if Tilda paid half as much attention to Poppy's Place as she did to her phone, she could be so much more help. "Never mind. They all sound qualified. I'm not sure how Mum's going to choose between them."

"Maybe once they've been for an interview Mum can invite some of them back for a trial shift?" Tilda suggested. "So we can see how they get on with the cats and customers."

"That's a great idea!' said Isla. "I'll email to invite them all for an interview next Saturday."

"You'd better check with Mum first," Tilda warned.

"But she's still at work," Isla moaned. "And we need to get this sorted – we need help now." She typed a reply to the first applicant, hit send and began on the next one.

"At least send Mum a text to let her know," said Tilda.

Isla picked up her phone. There were three more texts from Grace and two from Bonnie about the Valentine's disco.

"Girls!" Gran called out from the kitchen. "Customers are going to be here soon. Are the tables laid?"

Tilda jumped up, quickly stuffing her phone into her pocket. "Come on, we'd better help Gran," she said. "But don't forget about texting Mum."

There was a shout from the hall and Milo ran into the conservatory in his wellies. "It's snowing!" he yelled excitedly.

"Put a coat on if you're going outside!" Gran called after him.

Isla watched from the warmth of the conservatory as Milo bounded outside followed by Dynamo and Roo. She laughed as Roo stood on his back legs, batting at snowflakes as they swirled round him.

Poppy meowed from her spot on the windowsill. "Don't you want to play outside, too?" Isla asked her.

Poppy meowed again and jumped down to settle on one of the beanbags.

"I don't blame you," Isla said with a yawn. "I think I could do with a cat-nap, too."

"Come on, Isla!" Tilda moaned as she laid the tables. "You're supposed to be helping. Did you text Mum?"

"Oh, I forgot!" Isla said. She started writing a text, but every time she tried to type a word, a new text appeared from Grace or Bonnie.

"Isla!" Gran called. "Can you help me make the sandwiches?"

"Coming!" Isla called back, leaping to her feet.

*I'll text Mum later,* she thought.

Chapter
Six

"Where are my wellies?" Milo yelled on Sunday morning.

"What do you need wellies for?" Isla asked. She popped some bread in the toaster, then quickly tiptoed across the kitchen floor, leaping on to one of the swivel chairs at the counter. "It's freezing!"

"For the snow!" Milo told her.

"Ah…" Gran opened the blind in the kitchen. "I'm not sure you'll need them."

Isla and Milo followed Gran's gaze. The snow was all but gone, leaving muddy wet patches across the lawn.

"I wanted to build a snow fort for the cats!" Milo wailed.

Gran gave Milo a hug. "You wouldn't have had time anyway," she told him. "It's Sunday – your swimming gala is today."

In an instant, Milo forgot his disappointment about the snow and started bouncing around the kitchen. Then he paused. "You are all going to come and watch me, aren't you?"

Isla smiled. "We wouldn't miss it! Besides, Mum promised that we could go out for dinner afterwards as a treat."

"You certainly all deserve it – everyone's been working so hard for Poppy's Place," Mum said, as she joined them in the kitchen.

"But who'll look after the customers?" Milo asked.

"Poppy's Place is closed for the day!" Tilda sang, appearing in the doorway. "I can't wait! I've got so many plans! I'm going to go shopping with Gabriella and maybe try that new—"

Mum coughed loudly and jerked her head towards Milo.

"What?" Tilda asked.

"It's Milo's swimming gala, remember?" Isla hissed.

"Do I really have to come?" she whispered.

"I can hear you, you know!" Milo said, folding his arms. He pointed to his hearing aid. "I turned it up so that I have supersonic hearing!"

Mum frowned. "I'm not sure you should do that, Milo. It might hurt your ears." She glanced over at Tilda. "And to answer your question – yes, you do have to come. We are going to have a lovely family day out." She looked down at Benny who was trying to climb up her leg. "No cats allowed, I'm afraid, Benny."

Benny gave a small meow and padded off to lie beneath the radiator next to Oliver. Oliver let out a half-hearted growl, then readjusted himself so that he had his back to Benny.

Isla smiled. "I think Benny's got a crush!"

Tilda snorted. "I'm not sure Oliver feels the same way."

Isla finished her toast then ran to her
bedroom to get dressed. She loved the cats
and Poppy's Place, but she couldn't wait to
have a day that didn't involve waiting on tables
or homework. She'd finally completed the
profiles for Dolly's cats and had uploaded all
the information about the Cat-tacular. She
was also secretly a little bit glad to have a
break from Bonnie and Grace and their
constant questions about the Valentine's disco.
Had she chosen an outfit? What was she
doing with her hair? What colour nail varnish
was she going to wear? Was she going to ask
anyone to go with her? Who did she hope
might ask her? Isla knew that she should
probably feel excited about all that stuff,
but she had too much on her mind with the
Cat-tacular – that was far more important
than a disco.

Isla couldn't remember when she'd last had a more perfect day. Although the weather was still freezing, the Palmers had made the most of their day off. After Milo's swimming gala, they had visited all their favourite places in the city – the huge park, the toy shop and, finally, their favourite Italian restaurant where they'd stuffed themselves with pasta.

"Look at my medal!" Milo said to the hundredth person they passed on the way home.

"I don't think everyone needs to see your medal, Milo!" Tilda hissed, covering her face with her hair to avoid being recognized by anyone she knew.

"I think it's great!" Isla told Milo. "You were amazing."

"I can't believe you came second!" Mum

gushed, as she leaned to kiss Milo on the cheek. "I'm so proud of you!"

"Muuum!" Milo moaned, scrubbing his cheek. "I can't wait to show Dynamo! Can he sleep in my room tonight – as a special treat?"

Mum frowned. "If you let him sleep in your room once, he'll want to do it all the time."

Isla glanced at Milo and gave him a little smile. Milo had already been sneaking Dynamo into his bedroom every night anyway. Somehow, Dynamo knew to go back downstairs every morning before Mum woke up. Cats really were amazing animals, Isla thought.

"Pleaaaasse?" Milo begged. "You let Benny sleep on your bed."

"I do not!" Mum said.

Gran turned to give Mum a pointed look.

"Well … maybe I did once or twice after Benny's kittens had left," Mum admitted.

"To make sure Benny wasn't feeling lonely."

"So is that a yes?" Milo asked hopefully.

"OK," Mum agreed as they reached the house. "Just this once."

Isla's teeth chattered as Mum rummaged around in her bag looking for the door key.

"There'll be a frost in the morning," Gran said, pulling her coat round her.

Milo blew out hot puffs of air, making small clouds in front of him. "Maybe it will snow so much that I'll have to have a day off school!"

Gran shook her head. "It's too cold for snow."

"I've never understood that," Tilda said. "How can it be too cold to snow?"

"Actually," Isla said, "it can't be too cold to snow, but it can be too dry. When it's very cold, there's less moisture in the air, and so less chance of it snowing."

Tilda stared at Isla.

"What?" Isla asked. "I learned about it in science last week."

"I didn't think that you paid much attention to anything that wasn't cat related," Tilda joked.

"Finally!" Mum said, pulling her door key from the bottom of her handbag. "The cats must be starving."

"Listen," said Tilda, cocking her head to one side. "Can anyone else hear that noise?"

"It sounds like … running water," Isla said. "Like a tap is running or—"

"Oh no!" cried Mum, opening the front door.

She jumped back as water rushed out of the house and spilled on to the path.

"The cats!" Isla yelled. She pushed past Mum and splashed through the ankle-deep water into the hall.

"Don't turn on the lights!" Mum shouted. "It might not be safe."

Mum, Gran and Tilda followed, all of them calling out the cats' names. Milo ran upstairs shouting for Dynamo.

Isla saw a tiny grey blur in the garden in the darkness, quickly followed by two black blurs. "Roo, Ash and Ace are in the garden," Isla shouted.

"I can't find Dynamo!" Milo cried, hurrying

back downstairs.

"He's probably outside with the others," Isla reassured him.

"I'll see if he's in my room," Tilda said.

"I've turned off the water at the mains," Mum called from the kitchen. "I think we've got a burst pipe."

"Benny's hiding under my bed," Tilda called. "No sign of Dynamo, though."

Gran pulled out her phone. "I'll see if I can get hold of a plumber."

Isla went in to the kitchen in search of more cats. "Oh, Oliver!" she cried, lifting the old ginger cat from a large puddle beneath the radiator. "Why didn't you go outside?"

Mum grabbed a tea towel and took Oliver from Isla, rubbing at his damp fur.

"I've found an emergency plumber," Gran called coming into the kitchen. "And these, too."

She handed Isla one of the torches she was holding. "He'll be here in thirty minutes. We'd better start moving the furniture."

Isla followed after Gran with her torch, to see how far the damage had spread.

"It must have been leaking for a good few hours," Gran said as she and Isla looked around.

The water had seeped from the kitchen into the hall, which was completely waterlogged, and from there into the lounge. The carpet in the lounge squelched beneath Isla's feet and when they looked in the conservatory, Isla couldn't hold back the tears.

"It's ruined!" she cried as she shone the torch around and saw the full extent of the damage. "Poppy's Place is ruined."

There was water everywhere. It had already started to soak into the sofas and up the table

legs. The beanbags were sodden, and the cats'
toys and beds that had been on the floor were
damaged beyond repair.

"Oh, Isla," Gran said, giving Isla a hug.
"What a terrible thing to have happened."

There was a little meow from the garden.
Isla wiped away her tears and looked up.
Poppy was sitting on the windowsill, batting
at the window.

Isla pushed open the cat flap and Poppy poked her head through, sniffing at the water. "It's OK," Isla told her, picking her up to give her a cuddle.

"Dynamo's gone!" Milo wailed, running into the conservatory. "He's run away!"

Mum came into the conservatory, holding Oliver wrapped in a large fleecy blanket as though he were a baby.

"Don't worry, Milo, we'll find Dynamo," she said. "I'm sure he won't have gone far."

Suddenly Isla gasped. "What are we going to do about The Great Cat-tacular?"

Mum cast her eyes around the room. "I'm sorry, Isla, but I don't think there's going to be a Cat-tacular."

Chapter
Seven

When Isla woke up the next morning, she felt more exhausted than she had before she'd gone to bed. Luckily the plumber had managed to replace the broken pipe without too much difficulty. Then they'd moved most of the furniture upstairs and brushed the remaining water outside with brooms. Mum had found some old cardboard boxes and blankets, which they'd taken upstairs and made into makeshift beds for the cats. Isla had

Ash, Ace and Roo in her bedroom but they'd ignored the boxes to sleep on the end of her bed in a big pile of fluff.

Isla climbed out of bed and wandered on to the landing, banging her shin on the kitchen chairs that were stacked outside her door.

"Ow!" she winced, rubbing at her leg.

"I want Dynamo!" Milo wailed from downstairs.

Isla hurried down to the kitchen, where she found Gran and Mum trying to comfort Milo.

"Still no sign?" Isla asked quietly.

Gran shook her head.

"I'm sure he's OK, honey," Mum told Milo. "He probably got a bit scared by all the water and went somewhere to hide. He'll soon come back when he gets hungry."

Isla nodded. "And he's microchipped, so if someone finds him before we do, they'll know where he lives."

"I don't want to go to school," Milo sobbed, tears running down his cheeks. "I want to look for Dynamo."

"I'm sure he'll be back by the time you get home," Mum said. "And if he's not, then we can all go out and search together, OK?"

"I can make some posters," Isla suggested. "We can give them to the neighbours and ask them to look out for Dynamo."

Milo sniffed. "Promise we can look for him if he's not back by the time I get home?"

"I promise," Mum said, giving Gran a worried look.

Isla wandered into the conservatory, hoping that it had all been a bad dream and that Poppy's Place didn't look as bad as she remembered. She sighed when she saw all the damage again – in the daylight it actually looked worse. Mum had moved most of the café furniture outside, along with the cat beds and toys. It was all going to need replacing. Isla felt a sob rise in her chest.

The lounge wasn't as bad. Luckily the water had only soaked into part of the carpet and hadn't reached the sofas. The hall was a disaster, though – the carpet was soaked through and water had started to seep up the walls and into the wallpaper, leaving a horrible brown stain along the bottom.

"We're going to have to cancel all our bookings," Tilda told Isla as she came downstairs.

"All our hard work," Isla said. "Everything we did to get Poppy's Place up and running – to create somewhere special for cats and people. Now we're back to square one – worse even – square minus one hundred!"

"We did it before, we can do it again," Tilda said, giving Isla a hug.

"Not before Valentine's Day, though, in time for The Great Cat-tacular," Isla said glumly.

Tilda sighed. "No. Probably not. Let's just focus on getting Poppy's Place open again, then maybe we can reschedule the Cat-tacular when things are back to normal."

Isla stared at the floor. She didn't want to have the Cat-tacular another time. When

she'd visited Dolly's Farm, she had made a silent promise to herself and the cats that she would do her very best to find as many of them their forever homes as she could. She couldn't bear the thought that she'd let them all down.

"I've called Lucy to tell her I won't be at work today," Mum said, coming to join Isla and Tilda. "I need to call the insurance company and try to get someone round this morning. We can't make a start on any repairs until they've taken a look."

"Maybe we should stay home as well," Tilda said. "To help out?"

"Nice try," Mum said. "But you've got exams coming up. I know what has happened is awful but we need to carry on as normal – and for you three, that means going to school!"

Isla trudged slowly back upstairs to get ready.

"What a mess," she heard Mum mutter as she closed her bedroom door.

She quickly texted her friends to tell them she had terrible news, then she sat on the end of her bed and pulled a sleepy Roo into her chest to give him a hug. She buried her face in his warm fur and cried.

"Have you decided on your outfit yet?" Grace asked Isla at lunchtime.

Isla shook her head and put her sandwich away. She felt too sick to eat.

"I got your text!" Bonnie said, as she hurried over to join them. "What's the terrible news?"

Grace frowned and pulled out her phone, then she turned pink. "Sorry, Isla. I didn't see this. What's happened?"

Isla took a deep breath. She could hardly bear to think about it, let alone say it out loud. "We had a burst pipe at home," Isla said. "The house flooded and Poppy's Place is ruined."

"Oh no!" said Grace.

"And Dynamo's gone missing," said Isla, fighting back the tears.

"I'm so sorry," Bonnie said. "Is there

anything we can do?"

Isla shook her head. "Mum's promised that we can go and look for Dynamo if he's still not back when we get home from school. The café's going to take a while to dry out and we're going to have to start again from scratch. The Cat-tacular is cancelled as well."

Isla sighed. Mum had called Dolly on Sunday night to let her know the bad news. She hadn't said how Dolly had reacted but Isla knew she must have been disappointed.

"We'll be there when you need us, won't we, Bonnie?" Grace said, giving Isla a hug.

"Definitely." Bonnie grinned.

The girls were silent for a while as they ate their lunch, then Bonnie and Grace returned to their favourite topic – the Valentine's disco.

"Do you want to come clothes shopping with us?" Grace asked.

Bonnie nodded. "It might take your mind off things?"

Isla shrugged and bit her lip to hold back the tears. She couldn't stop thinking about Dynamo. She hoped that he was safely back at home by now. Isla didn't know how Milo would react if Dynamo wasn't there. She couldn't help remembering Millie, the cat Mum had had when she was a girl. Millie had gone missing and never returned.

Isla crossed her fingers, hoping that history wasn't going to repeat itself.

Isla ran all the way home from school. By the time she reached the front door she was gasping for breath.

"Any ... sign ... of ... Dynamo?" she panted

as she burst into the kitchen.

"I'm afraid not," said Gran. "Milo has been out in the garden, calling for him ever since he got home. Your mum's popped out to pick up a dehumidifier to dry out the walls. She's promised Milo that we'll all go out and look for Dynamo when she gets home."

"I'm going now," Isla said. "He can't have gone far!"

"Don't get your hopes up, Isla," said Gran.

"I'm going to find him, Gran," Isla said, determined. "I won't let Milo down."

Isla changed out of her uniform and headed across the street to the park opposite. She searched everywhere she could think of – under bushes, in trees. She even looked inside the tunnels in the playground in case Dynamo was hiding inside one of them.

"Have you lost something?" a voice said.

Isla jumped, banging her head on the metal roof. "I'm sure these tunnels used to be a lot bigger!" she huffed as she crawled out.

Sam grinned down at her. "I think maybe you used to be smaller."

"Dynamo's missing," Isla said, rubbing the back of her head.

"Your mum told my dad about the flood," Sam said. "Is there anything I can do?"

"You could help me look for Dynamo," Isla said, getting to her feet. "I've searched the park so maybe we can check with the neighbours."

They walked out of the park together in silence, looking around for the small tortoiseshell cat. Isla was sure that Sam grew another foot taller every time she saw him. She tried to think of something to say, but for some reason her mind was completely blank.

Finally, Sam spoke. "I … uh … I heard you were having a Valentine's disco at Langford High."

Isla rolled her eyes. "Not you as well!"

Sam gave Isla a confused look.

"It's all anyone is talking about at school," Isla told him. "How did you hear about it?"

"Ayesha's brother told me," Sam said.

"I think she feels a bit left out," said Isla. "I'm going to see if she's allowed to come, too."

"Oh," Sam said. "So you're not going with anyone?"

"I just said I was probably going to go with Ayesha…"

Sam blushed. "N-no…" he stuttered, "I meant—"

"Shh!" Isla said, looking round. "Did you hear that?"

Sam listened. "It sounds like a mouse."

They followed the noise to a bike shed in Mr Evans' front garden. "It's coming from inside," Isla said, her eyes wide.

She tapped gently on the side of the metal shed. "Dynamo!" she called.

Isla grabbed Sam's arm as there came a small meow in reply.

"It's him!" Isla cried.

She ran to Mr Evans' front door and knocked but there was no answer.

"How are we going to get Dynamo out?"
she asked Sam.

Sam went back to the shed and tried the
door. "It isn't locked," he said. "Should we go
in?"

Isla glanced around then nodded. Mr Evans'
car wasn't in the driveway. They could be
waiting hours until he came home. Dynamo
– and Milo – couldn't wait that long. Isla was
sure that Mr Evans wouldn't mind anyway.
The door creaked as Sam pulled it open.
Dynamo let out a little squeak and leaped into
Isla's arms.

"Milo is going to be so happy to see you!"
Isla cried, hugging Dynamo tightly. They
hurried back along the street. Isla paused
when they reached Sam's house. "Thank you!"
she said, glancing up at him.

Sam shrugged as his face turned pink again.

"No problem. Let me know if you need any help with … anything else."

Isla smiled then headed for home. She ran straight past Gran in the kitchen, who gave a little cry when she saw Dynamo in Isla's arms, and out into the garden where Milo was still calling for Dynamo over the back fence.

"Milo!" Isla called.

Milo ignored her.

"He's not wearing his hearing aid!" Gran said, coming outside and giving Dynamo a kiss on his head. "Where did you find him?"

"Just up the road. He was stuck inside Mr Evans' bike shed," Isla said.

"I wonder how he got in there?" Gran said.

"I'm not sure." Isla grinned. "I told you I'd find him."

"Thank goodness you did!" said Gran.

Isla walked to the end of the garden and

tapped Milo on the shoulder. Milo spun round.

"Dynamo!" he yelled.

Isla put her finger to her lips. "Don't scare him," she said.

"Sorry," Milo whispered.

Isla handed Dynamo over to Milo. She didn't think she'd ever seen someone look so happy.

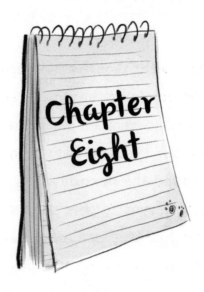

**Chapter Eight**

Poppy's Place: Important Update, Isla typed the following evening.

She wasn't able to help with the wet carpets or furniture, so Isla had decided that the most useful thing to do was update the website so people knew what was going on. Hopefully that way they wouldn't lose any customers – or potential cat owners.

Sad news at Poppy's Place, Isla continued. We arrived home late on Sunday evening to find that a burst pipe had flooded the whole of the downstairs. Luckily the cats were all safe and well – apart from our little runaway Dynamo, who was found the next day. Unfortunately, most of the conservatory will need drying out and redecorating before we can reopen for business.

Isla took a shaky breath and paused. She felt like she might cry again.

We would like to thank our customers for all their support so far and to reassure you that Poppy's Place will be open again as soon as possible.

She supposed that she should write something about The Great Cat-tacular being cancelled, as they'd already had quite a few people interested in attending, but she couldn't quite bear to. Writing it down would make it final, she thought. Finished. Isla just couldn't accept that. She still held on to the tiny hope that they might somehow still be able to hold the event. The insurance people had been during the day and told Mum that their claim could take a while. Until they had the money to replace everything that was lost, there wasn't much more they could do.

Isla clicked *upload* on her blog post and closed the laptop. Last night, she had made a plan to go into town with Mum at the weekend to buy some of things that needed replacing. Isla grabbed a piece of paper and started to make a list.

Things that need replacing:
Cat beds
Cat toys and scratching posts
Sofas
Beanbags

*Carpet in hallway and lounge*
*Wallpaper in hallway*

Luckily the kitchen floor was tiled and so it hadn't been damaged. Isla was surprised that apart from one cupboard door, the rest of the kitchen was OK as well. And they still had the coffee machine and all the crockery.

Isla gasped as an idea came into her head. They still had most of the *things* they needed for the Cat-tacular. The only part that was really ruined was the *venue*. What if they held the Cat-tacular somewhere else? Somewhere that was like Poppy's Place, where there were loads of cats – all waiting to be adopted.

Isla jumped off her bed and ran out on to the landing. "Family meeting!" she yelled. "Family meeting!"

"What's the matter, Isla?" Gran called from her room. She was sitting on her bed with a

♥ 113 ♥

cup of tea in one hand and a book in the other, with Poppy curled up at her feet.

"I've had the *best* idea!" Isla gasped, trying to catch her breath. She sat beside Poppy as Mum and Milo came in to join them.

"Where's Tilda?" Isla asked.

"I'm here!" Tilda huffed, as she appeared in the doorway. "Give me a chance!"

"So what's your big idea?" Gran asked as Poppy crawled on to her lap.

Tilda groaned. "You know that whatever it is, it's going to involve a lot of work for the rest of us."

Isla glared at Tilda, then continued. "It's about The Great Cat-tacular."

"I know you're disappointed," Mum said, "but there is really no way we can host it now. The house still needs to dry out, then there's decorating to be done and new furniture to buy, plus things for the cats."

"I know!" Isla said. "But we don't have to have the Cat-tacular at Poppy's Place."

Milo wrinkled his nose. "Then where?"

"We can have it at Dolly's Farm!" Isla told them. "I can't believe we didn't think of it to begin with – where better to have a cat adoption day than at an actual cat sanctuary?"

"I'm not sure, Isla," Mum said. "Even if Dolly agreed and we moved the Cat-tacular to her farm, there's still an awful lot of work to do."

Isla glanced over at Tilda and felt her heart drop. Tilda grinned back at Isla. "We can do it," she said. "I'll help Isla with everything for the Cat-tacular, and you and Gran can sort out the flood."

Isla gave Tilda a grateful smile. She didn't know why Tilda was being so nice, but she didn't care if it meant the Cat-tacular could still go ahead. Isla looked at Mum. "We'll do everything," she promised, crossing her fingers behind her back.

"Well," said Mum slowly. "Only if Dolly agrees…"

Isla grinned. "It'll be perfect! All the potential cat owners will actually be able to meet the cats and see if they get along – plus it gives us, and Lucy and Dolly, the chance to see how people interact with the cats and make sure they'd be suitable owners."

"What about food and drinks?" Gran asked.

"We can make everything here and take it to Dolly's – that way she wouldn't have to do a thing," Isla said.

"We *might* need a bit of help with the baking," Tilda said, looking hopefully at Gran.

"As long as I don't have to do it all," Gran agreed.

Tilda grinned. "Oh, and we could make bunting and take balloons to decorate the farm."

Isla beamed. "So what do you all think?"

One by one, they nodded in agreement.

"Brilliant!" Isla said. "Mum, could you call Dolly and see if she's OK with the idea?"

"Well, it's getting a bit late," Mum said, looking at her watch. "And I was just going to finish stripping the wallpaper—"

"Pleeeease!" Isla begged.

Mum sighed. "I promise I'll call first thing in the morning."

Isla jumped up from the bed and headed back to her room.

"Where are you going?" Mum called.

"To make new plans!" Isla said. "There's only two weeks until Valentine's Day!"

Chapter
Nine

"I'm going over to Grace's house," Isla told Gran when she got in from school on Friday afternoon.

"Can me and Dynamo come?" Milo called from the kitchen. "Dynamo misses his sister."

Grace had adopted Lady Mewington, one of Benny's kittens.

"Not this time, Milo," Isla said. "We've got loads of planning to do for the Cat-tacular. I'll take some pictures of Lady Mewington for you and Dynamo, though," she promised.

Mum hadn't spoken to Dolly about hosting the Cat-tacular yet but Isla was sure she'd say yes, so she'd asked her friends to help with everything they still needed to do.

Isla quickly got changed out of her school uniform and into her favourite pair of worn dungarees and a baggy jumper, then she grabbed her notebook and headed over to Grace's house.

"Where's your outfit?" Grace demanded as soon as she opened the front door with Lady Mewington tucked into the crook of her arm.

Isla looked down at her dungarees and scuffed trainers. "I'm … wearing it?"

Grace laughed and shook her head. "No, silly! Your outfit for the disco – we said we were going to try everything on, remember?"

Isla frowned. She didn't remember Grace

telling her that at all. She thought back to lunchtime, when Grace and Bonnie had been chatting about Valentine's Day. Isla had been so caught up in her plans for the Cat-tacular that she hadn't really been listening to their conversation.

"I might not have been paying attention," Isla said. "Sorry. Anyway, I thought you were going to help me with the plans for the Cat-tacular?"

"There's plenty of time to do both!" Grace said, ushering Isla up to her room. "Come on, you can try on some of my stuff."

"Wow!" Isla breathed, as she opened Grace's bedroom door. Bonnie and Ayesha were already there, sitting on Grace's huge bed, which was covered in clothes.

"I know," Ayesha said, rolling her eyes.

"What about this one?" Bonnie asked,

doing a little spin
in the middle of the
room to show off
the dark blue dress
she was wearing.

Grace nodded as
she placed a wriggly
Lady Mewington on
to the bed. "Put it on
the maybe pile."

Isla scooped up Lady
Mewington and sat next to
Ayesha, while Bonnie and Grace discussed
which colours went best with their hair.

"Have you been here long?" Isla asked
Ayesha as Lady Mewington jumped off her
lap and wriggled beneath a skirt on the floor.

"Not really," Ayesha replied. "But it feels
like *hours*. I thought we were meeting to talk

about the Cat-tacular, not the disco."

Isla gave Ayesha a hug and sighed. "Me, too. Do you want to hear about my plans so far?"

Ayesha nodded so Isla opened her notebook and started to read out her long list. She glanced up and caught Grace rolling her eyes at Bonnie. Her stomach did an uneasy flip but she continued anyway.

"We're going to make bunting," Isla said. "And blow up tons of balloons. Gran is helping us make cakes and sandwiches." Isla scanned her to-do list. "I still need to design some posters to advertise the new venue and the cat adoption application forms…" Isla paused. "I was hoping you might be able to come and help on the day – if you're free?"

"I'd love to," Ayesha said. "It's not like I've got any other plans for Valentine's Day."

Isla gasped. "Oh, Ayesha, I'm so sorry – with everything happening at Poppy's Place and the Cat-tacular I forgot to ask you if you wanted to come to the disco with me?"

Ayesha beamed at Isla. "Really? Are you allowed to bring guests who don't go to Langford High?"

Isla nodded. "I checked with Mrs Davies at school today and she said it's OK to bring a friend."

"You did?" Grace asked, turning bright pink. "Why didn't I think of that?"

Ayesha shrugged. "It's OK."

"Wait!" Grace cried, dropping the dress she was holding on top of Lady Mewington, who was now caught up in a pile of belts. "The Cat-tacular is on Valentine's Day?"

"Yes," Isla said. "I already told you that."

Grace and Bonnie exchanged a look. "But

that's the day of the disco," Bonnie said.

"So?" said Isla. "That's not until the evening. The Cat-tacular is during the day. There'll be plenty of time to do both."

"I'd love to help, Isla," Ayesha said.

Grace shook her head so hard that Isla felt a breeze from her hair. "But we need to *prepare!*"

"Prepare for what?" Isla asked, feeling thoroughly confused.

"We need to do our nails, and our hair and our makeup and have showers and make sure that everything is perfect!" Grace said in one big rush of words and air.

"Oh," Isla said. "Well, you don't have to help out at the Cat-tacular if you don't want to."

"It's not that we don't want to, Isla, but the disco is important, too!" Grace said.

"More important than cats finding homes?" Isla asked, feeling her face go hot.

"Yes, Isla!" Grace said. "We're not all as obsessed with cats as you are! We are allowed to be as excited about the disco as you are about cats."

Isla didn't know what to say. She stared at the floor as her eyes filled with tears. She thought about how fed up she'd felt every time Bonnie and Grace talked about the disco – maybe that's how they felt when she constantly talked about cats.

"There's no reason why we can't do both, is there, Grace?" Bonnie said quietly, looking between Grace and Isla.

Ayesha gave Bonnie a worried smile and nodded.

Grace crossed her arms and stared out of the window. "I'm not sure I want to now."

"I'm sorry," Isla said. "I didn't mean to be selfish – I just got a bit carried away. There's been so much going on with the Cat-tacular, and Poppy's Place and now the flood…" She wiped a hand across her face so that they wouldn't see her cry.

Grace squeezed herself on the bed between Isla and Ayesha and gave Isla a hug. "I'm sorry, too," she sniffed. "Of course we'll be there. I'm just looking forward to the disco so much. It's the first proper disco we've been to."

"We've been to loads of discos before." Isla laughed. "We went to one last month for Natalie's birthday."

"That doesn't count," Grace said. "It was at her house. This is a *proper* disco. And Mark has asked me to go with him." Grace blushed.

"Mark?" Isla asked.

"From drama club," Bonnie explained.

"I thought we were going to go together?" said Isla.

"We are!" Grace said.

Isla frowned. The whole *going with people to the disco* business was really confusing.

"Oh!" Grace gasped. "We could get ready

together here, before the disco?"

"Great idea!" Isla said. "We can come straight after the Cat-tacular."

"So what do you need us to do, Isla?" Bonnie asked.

Isla looked at her notebook. "Bonnie, can you help with refreshments?" she asked. "Ayesha and Grace can help Tilda at the front gate handing out name tags and registration cards."

"Sounds good to me," said Ayesha. "What will you be doing?"

Isla gave Ayesha a grateful smile. "I'll be pointing people in the right direction and handing out cat profiles," Isla said.

Grace laughed and rescued Lady Mewington from the pile of belts.

"Maybe we can come over tomorrow afternoon to help you with the bunting and posters?" Grace suggested.

Bonnie nodded. "If you need us?"

"I need all the help I can get!" Isla replied as her phone beeped. She pulled it out of her pocket and glanced at the screen. It was a text from her mum: *Dolly says OK!*

Isla grinned. "I knew Dolly would say yes!" she cried. "It looks like The Great Cat-tacular is on!"

As she started to write a reply to Mum, she noticed the unsent text from the other day. "Oh no! I forgot to tell Mum that I'd invited people to come for an interview for Poppy's Place."

"Can't you just rearrange the interviews?" Ayesha asked.

Isla frowned. "Maybe," she said slowly. She waved a hand in the air. "I'm sure it will be fine. I'll tell Mum when I get home."

# Chapter Ten

"Right," said Mum as she and Isla waited for the bus into town early on Saturday morning. "Our first priority is to get everything for the cats, then if we have time we can look for stuff for the house and anything we might need for the Cat-tacular. What's on your list, Isla?"

Isla looked at her list, which was scribbled on a torn piece of paper. The notebook Gran had bought her was full up, so Isla had had to make do with the first thing she could find, which just happened to be her maths book.

"I've got cat beds and one of those scratching posts if we can carry it," Isla read. "Plus some new toys. Then we need some wallpaper and maybe a rug to cover up the stain in the hallway?"

Mum groaned. They had ripped up the ruined carpet from the hall, hoping that the floorboards underneath would be good enough to leave bare, but there was a dark water stain from the front door right the way to the kitchen. "I'm not sure we can carry all of this on our own," Mum said. "Maybe we should leave the rugs and wallpaper for another time?"

"OK," Isla said, reading on. "For the Cat-tacular we need some colourful material and ribbon for the bunting, and some balloons – I wonder if we can find any with cats on?"

"We'll just have to see what we can get,"
Mum told her as the bus arrived.

They got on board and sat down, and Isla
folded up her list. "Oh, and I need a new
notebook," she said. "Preferably cat-themed."

Mum sighed. "Of course you do."

"At least Poppy's Place can reopen soon,"
Isla said. "That's great news!" The damage
hadn't been as bad as they'd first thought.
They'd hired a dehumidifier, which had
sucked up all the water and moisture from the
room, and they'd been able to clean up most of
the conservatory furniture.

Mum nodded. "If we can get everything for
the cats today, then maybe we can open the
week after the Cat-tacular," she said.

Isla smiled. Things were finally on track
again. She just hoped that plenty of people
would come to the Cat-tacular.

"We're home!" Mum called as she and Isla struggled through the front door, laden with bags and boxes.

"Did you get me anything?" Milo asked as he bounded down the hallway.

"Sorry, Milo," Mum said. "But we did get a new bed for Dynamo so he doesn't have to sleep in your bedroom any more."

"Ohhhhh!" Milo cried. "But he likes it in my room. He's made himself a little bed in the corner on top of my comics."

Mum opened her mouth to reply just as Gran appeared from the lounge. "Did you forget to tell us about something, Isla?" she asked slowly.

Isla dumped her bags on the floor and looked to Milo for some clue as to why Gran seemed so cross. Milo shrugged and sneaked off upstairs.

"Um…" Isla said, scratching her head. "Was I supposed to help bake something?"

Gran shook her head. "No." She looked at Mum. "We've had a couple of visitors this morning," she said. "All looking for you – about the job?"

Isla gasped and slapped her hand to her forehead. "The interviews! I can't believe I forgot to tell you – again!"

"Interviews?" Mum asked. "What inter—" She paused, seeing the sheepish look on Isla's face. "What have you done now, Isla?"

"I meant to tell you about it, I really did! It's just that we were all so busy with the Cat-tacular and Poppy's Place and then the flood. I *might* have invited some people to come for an interview for the Poppy's Place job – this morning."

"Oh, Isla!" Mum sighed. She looked at Gran. "What did you tell them?"

"Well, I couldn't just send them away, could I?" Gran said. "One lady had taken two trains and a bus to get here." She gave Isla a pointed look. "So I did the interviews myself."

"You did?" Isla asked. "What were they like? Were any of them any good?"

"They were all very nice," Gran said. "But it's up to your mum to make the final decision." She tutted. "You really should have told us about this, Isla. You'll be a teenager soon – that means taking more responsibility for things."

"I'm sorry," Isla said.

Gran held up her flowery notebook. "Well, I followed your lead and made notes on all of the candidates."

"Can I see?" Isla asked, reaching for the notebook.

"Maybe later," Mum said. "I'm going to make a start on painting the conservatory, and you and Tilda have got some bunting to sew." Mum looked round. "Where is Tilda?"

"She's gone over to Gabriella's," Gran said. "She said to tell Isla to start without her."

Isla huffed and picked up the bag full of colourful material and ribbons. She was halfway up to her room when there was a knock at the door.

"Who could that be now?" Gran wondered.

Mum opened the door to find a young woman who couldn't have been much older than Tilda standing on the doorstep. She had the curliest blond hair Isla had ever seen and wore a knitted woolly jumper with a cat on the front. Isla liked her immediately.

"Hello," said the woman. "I'm here for the interview. Sorry I'm a bit late. My cats wouldn't let me leave the house." She smiled at Isla. "They have a few separation anxiety issues," she whispered.

"Oh," said Mum. "I'm not sure…"

"Is that Poppy?" the woman said, crouching down to stroke Poppy as she wandered over to greet her. "She's beautiful."

The woman stood up and held out her hand to Mum. "I'm Leonora," she said, shaking Mum's hand. "I've read all about Poppy's Place and your wonderful cats on the website."

"I'll make some tea," Gran said, heading to the kitchen. "Isla, would you like to help me?"

"Oh, but I..." Gran gave Isla a look that said "don't argue" and Isla followed, while Mum took Leonora into the lounge.

"She seems nice, doesn't she, Gran?" Isla gushed as she cut a slice of chocolate cake to take to Leonora. "Did you see her jumper?"

Gran laughed. "I did."

"And she has her own cats," Isla continued. "So she's obviously a cat lover and knows how to take care of them properly."

"I'm sure she does," Gran said, pouring water from the kettle into the teapot.

Isla leaned her head round the kitchen door. "I wonder what they're talking about."

"Don't you have some bunting to make?" Gran reminded Isla.

"Yep," Isla said, resigned. "Although Tilda was supposed to help me!"

Isla picked up her bag and crept up to her room, straining to listen at the closed lounge door as she passed by.

A little while later, Isla heard the front door slam. She dropped her needle and thread and ran downstairs.

"How did it go?" she asked Mum excitedly. "She seemed great, didn't she? When can she start? You have to hire her!"

Mum laughed. "She seemed very nice. She

has waitressing experience and has three cats of her own, so she knows all about caring for cats."

"Are you going to offer her the job?" Isla asked.

"Well, we will be needing help as soon as we're up and running again," Mum admitted. "So, yes, I think I might … but I should speak to the other candidates first, just to be fair."

Isla whooped and jumped in the air as there was another knock at the door. She was still grinning when she opened the door to Ayesha, Bonnie and Grace.

"I've brought supplies!" Ayesha said, holding up two large bags full of colourful material and ribbons.

"Brilliant!" said Isla. "Come on up!"

The girls followed Isla up to her room and quickly got to work, cutting out piles of triangles. Then they began sewing them on to the lengths of ribbon.

"I went shopping with Mum this morning for a new dress for the disco," Ayesha told her friends. She paused. "It is still OK if I come, isn't it?"

Isla smiled. "It wouldn't be the same without you!"

Bonnie put down her sewing. "I have to tell you all something," she said, her face turning pink. "Someone has asked me to go to the disco with them – a boy," she added quickly.

"Ooh!" Grace squealed. "Who is it?"

"Jack," Bonnie said.

"Jack?" Isla repeated. "With the cockatiel?"

"Cockatiel?" Grace snorted. "Jack has a cockatiel?"

"I don't think he'll be bringing it with him!" Bonnie huffed.

Isla picked up her needle and continued sewing as her friends chatted excitedly about Bonnie's news.

*So much for Mum's ridiculous idea that Jack had a crush on me!* she thought. That must have been why he'd ignored her at the vets. Not because he liked Isla, but because he liked her

Chapter Eleven

The house was unusually quiet on Sunday morning. Mum had taken Milo to get his hair cut and Gran had gone to visit Mr Evans. There was no sign of Tilda – Isla guessed she hadn't made it out of bed yet. She was still feeling annoyed with Tilda for not helping out with the Cat-tacular like she'd promised.

At least she could rely on her friends, Isla thought as she looked at the pile of bunting they'd made yesterday. There was still so much to do, though. Isla picked up the new notebook she'd bought in town with Mum. She'd had a great new idea for a blog post.

Reasons to adopt a cat:

1. Cats are the most loving animals in the world. Whenever you are feeling sad, or having a bad day, a cat is always there to cheer you up.

2. Cats are independent. If you have a busy job or are away from home a lot, you don't need to worry about leaving your cat alone. Cats don't need taking for walks like dogs — if they want to go for a walk, they just go by themselves!

3. Cats are clever. You don't need to teach a cat how to heel or behave — they just do it! You won't come home to find that a cat has ripped up your sofa. Or that they've escaped from their cage. Cats are practically like humans, only smaller and furrier!

"What are you writing?" Tilda said, hovering in the doorway to Isla's bedroom.

"A new blog post," Isla said, shutting her notebook. "I thought it'd be useful to tell people why cats make such great pets."

Tilda raised her eyebrows. "That's a good idea."

"You don't have to sound so surprised!" Isla said, pulling a pink thread off her pillow from yesterday's sewing session.

Tilda picked up some of the material triangles laid out on Isla's bed. "I'll help you with this, if you like?"

"Well, we *are* supposed to be doing it together," Isla said.

As Tilda reached for some ribbon, her phone beeped. She picked it up to read the text and gave a little smile before tapping out a reply.

"I've only got time to help for a bit, though," said Tilda, tucking her phone in her pocket. "I'm going out later."

"But there's still so much to do!" Isla said. "Where are you going?"

Tilda blushed. "I'm going to the cinema," she said. "With a boy."

Isla gasped. "Is that who's been sending you those texts?" Suddenly it all made sense – the constant texts and giggling. Isla gave Tilda a sly grin. "Does Mum know?" she asked.

Tilda nodded quickly, then started frantically sewing a fabric triangle on to some ribbon.

"Who is he?" Isla asked. "Does he go to our school? What's his name? Have I met him before?"

Tilda glared at Isla. "None of your business!"

"Is this your first date?" Isla asked, trying not to giggle.

Tilda glanced up at Isla and sighed. "Stop distracting me, I'm trying to sew!"

The two girls worked away in silence, with Tilda muttering every time she stabbed herself with the needle.

"Tilda…" Isla said an hour later, after she'd sewn what felt like the hundredth triangle.

"Hmm?" Tilda asked, squinting as she tried to rethread her needle.

"Can I ask you a question?"

Tilda nodded. "As long as it's not about my date."

"It's this Valentine's disco," Isla said. "It seems like everyone in my year is going with someone."

"I thought you were going with Ayesha?" Tilda asked.

"I am, but…" Isla looked at the floor, suddenly wishing she'd never started the conversation.

"Ohhhhh," Tilda said, giving Isla a knowing look. "You mean that everyone is going with *someone*?" Isla nodded. "Just because you're not going with a boy, doesn't mean that you won't have a good time," Tilda said. "I bet you'll be with your friends most of the evening anyway."

"Really?" Isla asked. Ever since she'd found out that Bonnie was going with Jack, Isla had been worried that maybe she should have tried harder to find *someone* to go with, too. But she'd been so preoccupied with all the cat stuff going on that it hadn't seemed that important … until now.

"There *might* be someone who wants to go with you to the disco, if you're still interested?" Tilda teased.

Isla froze. "Who?"

"Leave it to me," Tilda sang. "I'll be your fairy godmother!"

"Tilda!" Isla shrieked, blushing. "Tell me who it is!"

There was a knock at the front door and Tilda squealed.

"Oh no!" she cried, jumping up. "He's here already! I didn't realize what time it was. Mason's here!"

Tilda glanced at herself in the mirror and smoothed down her hair.

"How do I look? Should I change my top? Oh, I don't have time!" She had another quick glance in the mirrror before hurrying downstairs. "Wish me luck!"

"Have fun!" Isla called after her. "I'll just carry on with this by myself … again," she said, picking up another triangle to sew on to her ribbon.

"There's still loads to do," Isla said, as her friends arrived that afternoon.

"What's that amazing smell?" Bonnie asked, inhaling deeply.

"Gran's already started baking," Isla said. "She's trying out some new recipes for the Cat-tacular – she said we could taste them later when we help out."

Bonnie and Grace grinned at each other.

"I can't wait!" said Bonnie.

"But first we need to make posters and a big sign to put up at the entrance to Dolly's Farm so that people know where to go. We've already put a notice on the website and at Abbey Park Vets to advertise the event. Tilda even managed to get an advert in the *Abbey Park Chronicle*," Isla told them. "And we've got some flyers to hand out to advertise Poppy's Place as well."

"Why don't we each make a poster? Then we can all work on the sign for the farm together," Ayesha suggested. "And after that we can get on with the important job of helping your gran with the tasting!"

Isla nodded and the girls followed her into the conservatory, where she'd laid out big sheets of paper, card and an assortment of pens.

"Where's Tilda?" Bonnie asked as she wrote *The Great Cat-tacular* in huge swirly letters across the top of one of the pieces of paper. "I thought she was supposed to be helping."

"That looks amazing!" Isla told Bonnie. "Tilda *was* supposed to be helping." Isla grinned. "But she's gone on a date."

"Ooh! With who?" Ayesha asked.

"Someone from school, I think," Isla said. "Mason?"

Grace gasped. "Mason Moretti? He's so cool!" she said, pretending to swoon.

Isla crinkled her nose. "Whoever it is, Tilda seems to find him hilarious – and they're always texting each other."

The girls worked on, chatting away about the Cat-tacular. No one noticed Gran appear in the doorway an hour later.

"You're doing a great job, girls," she said. "Would now be a good time to come and help me with the baking?" she asked. "And the tasting!"

All four girls grinned. "Yes, please!" said Grace. "Especially the tasting part!"

The girls trooped into the kitchen, breathing in the delicious scents of cinnamon and freshly baked bread.

"We need to make as many cakes and buns as we can fit in the freezer," Gran told them. "So we don't have too much to do on the big day." She handed them each a bowl of dough.

"I thought we were just taste-testing?" Isla asked.

Gran shook her head. "I said that *I'd* help *you*, Isla. Not the other way around."

Isla looked at her friends and laughed. "We'd better start kneading!" she said.

Two hours later, they were all exhausted. Isla hadn't realized how hard baking was. There seemed to be more flour on the kitchen counters, the floor and themselves than they'd put in the actual cakes. But they had made enough buns and cakes to fill the freezer, and that meant Isla could cross something else off her long list.

"I'm starving!" Grace groaned.

Ayesha glanced at the oven. "It all smells so good."

"Can we eat one now?" Isla asked Gran as she brushed more flour out of her hair.

Gran smiled. "I think you've earned it."

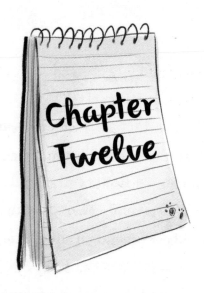

Chapter
Twelve

"Today is the day!" Isla squealed as she ran
around gathering up everything they needed.
"The Great Cat-tacular is finally here!"

"Are we ready?" Mum asked, standing by
the front door with a mountain of bags.

"I think so," Isla said, checking her list for
the hundredth time. "Did you pack the
balloons?"

Mum sighed. "Yes, Isla. And the bunting,
and the T-shirts and Poppy's Place flyers.

They haven't suddenly jumped out of the bags since the last time you asked!"

"Sorry," Isla said. "I just want everything to be perfect, so that we find as many cats their forever homes as possible."

Mum gave Isla a hug. "I'm sure we will," she said. "But whatever happens, you should be very proud of yourself. You and Tilda have done an amazing job pulling all of this together – especially with everything else that's been going on."

"Eeeeeeeeee!" Tilda screamed, as she ran down the hallway to pick up the post. She flipped through the letters, which were mostly brown envelopes, until she found a large red envelope. She turned it over and squealed again. "It's for me!"

Isla looked at Mum and rolled her eyes. "I need you to focus today, Tilda," Mum said.

"You can swoon over Mason later."

Tilda blushed. "Have you got your outfit for the disco, Isla?" she asked.

Isla gasped. "I almost forgot!" She ran upstairs to fetch it.

"Lucy should be here soon," Mum said, glancing out of the lounge window.

There was far too much for them to take on the bus to Dolly's Farm, so Lucy had volunteered to pick them up in her van. Unfortunately there was only room for three people in the front, so Tilda, Milo and Gran were going to catch the bus.

"Are you dressed yet, Milo?" Gran called up the stairs. "We need to get going."

"Coming!" Milo yelled. He appeared at the top of the stairs with his hands on his hips, wearing the Catboy outfit Gran had made him. "I'm ready to save the cats!"

"I am not getting on the bus with Milo looking like that!" Tilda said. "Someone might see me!"

"You mean Mason?" Milo teased, as he made kissing noises at Tilda.

"Make him stop!" Tilda cried.

Outside, a van beeped.

"That's Lucy!" Mum said. "Ready, Isla?"

Gran handed Isla a stack of cake tins and Isla carefully made her way along the icy path to Lucy's van.

"Hi, Isla!" Sam called from his front garden.

Isla peered over the top of the cake tins and smiled. "Hi, Sam."

"I'll see you later?" Sam asked.

Isla frowned. "Are you coming to the Cat-tacular?"

"Yes… If that's OK?"

"I guess so," Isla replied. She hadn't thought that the Cat-tacular would be of interest to Sam.

They reached Dolly's Farm in no time and Isla got straight to work, hanging the sign on the front gate and threading the bunting around the stables and the alpacas' enclosure. Isla hoped that they wouldn't eat the bunting before the guests arrived.

Dolly had put out tables for the refreshments

and there was another table by the front gate with registration forms for all the visitors. Lucy was setting up nearby, with leaflets about looking after cats and some flyers for Abbey Park Vets.

Isla jumped up and down to keep warm. It was bitterly cold but she didn't want to do up her coat because she wanted everyone to see her Poppy's Place T-shirt.

"At least it's not snowing," she said. "That might have put people off coming."

"Or raining," Mum added. "I've had enough of wet feet to last me a lifetime."

"Ah, look, here's Tilda, Gran and Milo," said Mum, pointing towards the drive.

"At last," said Isla. "I was getting worried!" She directed them straight to the refreshment table to set up the cakes and hot drinks.

A few minutes later, Ayesha, Bonnie and

Grace arrived, and they made a start on blowing up the balloons and arranging them in colourful bundles.

Isla checked her watch and glanced around, making sure that everything was ready. It was almost ten o'clock. "Where is everyone?" she said anxiously. "People should be arriving by now."

Suddenly Isla spotted a familiar figure walking up the drive. "Mr Black!" Isla said, waving at him.

Mr Black was a health inspector and a huge cat lover. He'd helped the Palmers' get Poppy's Place up and running and had come to the opening party.

"Are you looking for a cat?" Isla asked.

Mr Black nodded. "I've moved to a new house," he said. "Which means that I can finally adopt a cat."

"That's brilliant news!" Isla said. She
already knew that Mr Black would make a
great cat owner. She handed him a copy of the
cat profiles. "All the cats are on here," she told
him. "Dolly can show you around if you'd like
to meet any of them."

Dolly stepped forwards to introduce herself,
and she and Mr Black headed off in the
direction of the barn.

Slowly more and more people arrived. Isla handed out cat flyers and pointed people towards the refreshments. She was just returning to the desk for more flyers when she felt a tap on the shoulder.

"Hi, Isla," Leonora said, as Isla spun round. "Your mum said it would be OK if I popped by. Do you need any help?"

"Yes, please," Isla said, relieved to see Leonora, as another large group of visitors

turned up. "I was worried that there might not be enough people here. Now I'm worried there might be too many!"

She looked over at Gran, Bonnie and Milo at the refreshment table. The queue was huge.

"I'll help your gran with the cakes," Leonora said.

Isla nodded gratefully and smiled to herself. She was certain Leonora was going to fit in really well at Poppy's Place.

Isla picked up another pile of flyers and cat profiles and handed them out as she walked around the farm, answering questions and telling people as much as she could about each cat.

As she skirted round the alpacas' pen, Isla felt another tap on her shoulder. "Can I have a flyer?"

She turned round to see Sam grinning at her.

"Do you want to adopt a cat?" Isla asked, handing him a flyer and the cat profiles.

"Uh … I'm not sure my mum would let me," Sam said. "But I do like cats. Maybe I can hang out at Poppy's Place sometime instead?" he asked.

Before Isla could answer, Mum called her away to help at the refreshment table.

"Sorry," Isla said. "Got to go!"

"Maybe I'll see you later?" Sam called after her.

Isla nodded and hurried over to Mum.

"Could you refill these for me?" Mum asked, handing Isla two large water jugs.

As Isla headed for the kitchen, she bumped into Mr Black coming out of the barn. "Have you seen any cats that you might like to adopt yet?" Isla asked.

"There are some lovely cats here," Mr Black said. He glanced over at Dolly, who was introducing a small group of people to the alpacas. "Dolly is doing an amazing job looking after all these animals." He paused. "But I'm not sure I've found the right cat for me."

"Oh," Isla said, trying not to sound too disappointed. She had been certain that

Mr Black would adopt one of Dolly's cats.

"The thing is," Mr Black continued, "I was hoping to find a cat like the one I used to have when I was a boy. He was a beautiful black cat with green eyes."

"Would you be open to taking in more than one cat?" Isla asked, an idea forming in her head. "If you found the right ones?"

"Maybe," said Mr Black.

"Could you pop in to Poppy's Place tomorrow?" Isla asked excitedly. "We have two cats I think you'd love."

By four o'clock, Isla's feet were throbbing. They'd almost run out of cake, and she'd handed out all of her flyers and cat profiles. As the last of the visitors made their way out of the gates, she went to find Dolly, who was having a well-earned cup of tea with Lucy, Gran and Tilda.

"How did it go?" Isla asked, crossing her fingers for luck.

"Brilliant!" Lucy said, sipping her tea.

Gran poured Isla a cup and handed it to her with a smile.

"Better than brilliant," Dolly said. "I still have to do a few checks but I think we've managed to find eight cats their forever homes."

Isla gasped in amazement. "Eight cats! I can't believe it!"

"That's fantastic!" Tilda mumbled with a mouth full of cookie.

"The best part is that I won't have to turn away any new arrivals," Dolly said. "Although I do need to be sensible about the number of cats I can take on in the future."

Isla was so happy she thought she might burst. "Wait!" she said. "Make that ten cats – I think I may have found the perfect home for Ash and Ace. Maybe we should have a Cattacular every month?" Isla suggested.

"Let's not get carried away!" Mum laughed, as she and Milo joined them.

Grace, Bonnie and Ayesha hurried over. "Are you ready to go?" Grace called excitedly. "My dad's here to take us back to mine."

"I almost forgot!" Isla said. "The Valentine's disco!"

"How could you forget!" Bonnie squealed. "I've been looking forward to it since Christmas."

"I know," Isla said, rolling her eyes and laughing.

Three hours later, and after multiple last-minute outfit changes, they were all dressed and ready to go. Isla had borrowed one of Tilda's old dresses – it was green with tiny diamantes sewn into the bodice, and Grace had styled Isla's hair into soft curls. Tilda had offered Isla a pair of high-heeled shoes as well, but Isla didn't think she'd be able to walk in them, let alone dance, so she'd worn her trainers and some sparkly tights.

"You all look very grown up," said Grace's dad, making a pretend sniffle.

"Da-aad!" Grace groaned. "Don't start crying – honestly!"

The sound of the door bell saved the girls from any more embarrassment. Grace hurried to answer it and found Mark, Jack and Sam on the doorstep. Sam was dressed in a shirt and smart trousers, and holding a rose.

Grace squealed and turned to Isla.

"Sam?" Isla said. "What are you doing here?"

"I ... uh ... Tilda told me you were here and I was wondering... I should have asked sooner, but there didn't seem to be the right time. Anyway, some of my friends are going to the disco at your school as well, and so I wondered if…" He broke off suddenly, looking as though he'd made a terrible mistake.

"You wanted to ask Isla to go to the disco with you?" Grace blurted out.

Isla blinked. "You did?" she asked. "You do?"

Sam looked up at Isla and nodded. "Would you?"

Isla felt her face turn crimson. "I … I suppose…" She looked back at Ayesha. "Oh, but I said I'd go with Ayesha."

"That's OK," Ayesha smiled. "We can all go together."

Isla turned back to Sam. "Well, I guess…"

Grace rolled her eyes. "She says yes!" she said, pushing Isla out of the door and grabbing Mark's arm. "Come on, we're going to be late!"

Bonnie, Jack and Ayesha hurried after her.

Isla glanced up at Sam. He handed her the rose and she gave him a shy smile, finally starting to understand what all the fuss was about.

Chapter
Thirteen

Isla woke up on Sunday morning feeling like
yesterday had been a dream. An amazing,
perfect dream. Her feet were aching from the
Cat-tacular and the disco, where she'd danced
with her friends all night. Tilda had been
right – even though they'd gone together, the
girls had stuck together on one side of the hall
while the boys stayed on the other.

Grace had been the only one who'd actually
danced with a boy but Isla didn't mind.

Eventually the boys and girls had all danced together in one big group. Isla looked over to her bedside table where she had put the rose Sam had given her in a glass of water, and smiled again. She dragged herself out of bed and shuffled downstairs into the kitchen.

"How was the disco?" Gran asked.

"It was so much fun," Isla said.

"Told you," Tilda said, giving her a wink over the top of her latte. "And how was your not-so-secret admirer?"

"What's this?" Mum asked.

"Nothing!" Isla said quickly, giving Tilda an evil glare and willing her to keep quiet.

Tilda grinned and took another sip of her coffee.

"Have we had any more interest in the cats at Dolly's Farm?" Isla asked, trying to change the subject.

Mum nodded. "Dolly called me last night while you were at the disco to say that she has had a few calls from people who couldn't make it to the Cat-tacular but who were interested in adopting a cat."

"That's great news!" Isla beamed.

There was a knock at the door and Mum jumped up to answer it. "That'll be Leonora," she said. "I asked her to come in for training before we reopen next weekend."

"We got some more bookings for Poppy's Place at the Cat-tacular as well," Tilda said. "So it should be business as usual next Saturday."

"Not quite," Gran said. "Milo and I are

going to have a day off."

"We're going to the zoo!" Milo mumbled with a mouth full of cereal.

Mum showed Leonora into the kitchen and explained where they kept everything for the cat café. "Tilda can give you a coffee machine tutorial," Mum said.

Leonora glanced at the coffee machine. "Oh, I've used that one before."

"I told you she was perfect!" Isla whispered to Mum.

Mum grinned. "Could you introduce Leonora to the cats?"

"That's Oliver," Isla said, pointing to the snoring cat beneath the radiator. "He's really old and pretty much lives on that one warm spot."

Isla took Leonora into the conservatory and pointed out the cat playground in the garden. She was glad to see that the snow and slush had finally cleared and the sun was shining. She'd had enough of cold, wet feet.

"This is Roo," Isla said as he scurried past and made a dive for the cat flap, swiftly followed by Ash and Ace.

She wandered over to the sofa. "This is Benny, and this is her son, Dynamo."

"Oh, they're so cute!" Leonora cooed, kneeling down to stroke the cats. Poppy walked over and sat behind her, giving a little meow.

Isla laughed. "And you've already met Poppy."

"Hi, Poppy," Leonora said, holding her hand up to Poppy. Poppy batted at it in a cat high-five and Leonora smiled. "What a clever cat!"

Isla showed Leonora the menus and where they kept the cats' toys. "We do have some rules, because it's just as important that the cats are happy and healthy as it is that the customers have a good time."

Leonora nodded. "I visited a cat café in Japan when I was travelling for my gap year," she said. "But this is way more impressive."

"Really?" Isla said.

"Definitely," Leonora replied. "I love that Poppy's Place is about finding homes for cats rather than just making money. You've got something really special here."

Isla glanced around at the newly decorated café and how happy the cats looked.

"Isla," Gran called from the kitchen. "We've got another visitor."

"Why don't I get to know the cats for a bit?" Leonora suggested.

Isla left Leonora chatting to Poppy and hurried into the kitchen, where she found Gran pouring Mr Black a cup of tea.

"Mr Black said you invited him over," Gran said.

"I meant to tell you!" Isla said in a rush. "I just—"

"Forgot?" Gran finished with a smile. "No wonder you're always writing everything in those notebooks of yours. It seems to be the only way you can remember."

Isla blushed. "There's always so much to remember."

"Isla is never happier than when she's making plans," Gran told Mr Black.

"Well," said Mr Black, taking a sip of his tea, "who was it that you wanted me to meet?"

"Come with me," Isla said, gesturing for Mr Black to follow her out to the garden.

They sat outside and watched as Roo, Ash and Ace chased each other across bridges and through the tunnels that Sam and Mr Evans had built.

Mr Black sat silently for so long that Isla started to wonder if she might have made a mistake. Just as she was about to break the silence, Mr Black turned to her with a huge smile on his face. "They're perfect!" he said. "I'd love to give Ash and Ace a home."

"You would?" Isla asked, barely able to contain her excitement. "Both of them?"

Mr Black nodded. "It would be a shame to separate them."

"Oh, it really would!" Isla said, grinning from ear to ear.

Isla noticed Mum in the conservatory, talking with Leonora. "Mum!" she called, waving at her.

"What's the big emergency?" Mum said, coming outside.

Isla looked at Mr Black and grinned. "Ash and Ace have found their forever home!"

"That's wonderful!" Mum turned to Mr Black. "You've got yourself two adorable cats!"

Isla let out a contented sigh. Poppy's Place was going to reopen. The Cat-tacular had been a spectacular success and they'd found a forever home for Ash and Ace, too. She gasped as she suddenly realized the very best thing of all.

"You know what this means, don't you?" Isla said, looking up at Mum.

"Oh no," Mum groaned. "I know that look, Isla Palmer and it usually only means one thing."

Isla laughed. "We're going to need some new cats for Poppy's Place."

# KATRINA CHARMAN

Katrina lives in south-east England with her husband and three daughters. She has wanted to be a children's writer ever since she was eleven, when she was set the task of writing an epilogue to Roald Dahl's *Matilda*. Her teacher thought her writing was good enough to send to Roald Dahl himself. Sadly Katrina never got a reply, but the experience ignited her love of reading and writing.

Tweet Katrina: @katrinacharman

## LUCY TRUMAN

Since graduating from Loughborough University
with a degree in Illustration, Lucy has become one
of the UK's leading commercial illustrators. Lucy
draws inspiration from popular culture, fashion and
all things vintage to create her fabulous artworks.
This, combined with her love of people-watching,
allows Lucy to create illustrations which encapsulate
aspirational everyday living.

Tweet Lucy: @iLucyT

Find out how Poppy's Place got started...

# Poppy's Place

### THE HOME-MADE
## CAT CAFÉ

ILLUSTRATED BY
## LUCY TRUMAN

## KATRINA CHARMAN

Poppy's Place
Trouble
AT THE
CAT CAFÉ
ILLUSTRATED BY
LUCY TRUMAN
PAINT
KATRINA CHARMAN

# Poppy's Place

Cat café or total CAT-ASTROPHE?

Join in the fun at
**#POPPYSPLACE**
Tweet @stripesbooks